THE UNREAD LETTER

A PRIDE & PREJUDICE VARIATION

KARA PLEASANTS

Quills & Quartos
PUBLISHING

ISBN 978-1-951033-74-3 (ebook) and 978-1-951033-75-0 (paperback)

Edited by Justine Rivard and Regina McCaughey-Silvia

Cover Design by Ellen Pickels

On the cover *A Favor*, 1898, Edmund Blair Leighton, and *Brighton Beach looking west,* ca. 1824-28, John Constable

To Mom, Grandma Ann, and Grandma Sharon—for always believing in me

CONTENTS

IN THE HEAT OF THE MOMENT

*E*lizabeth awoke to the same thoughts and meditations which had at length closed her eyes–Mr Darcy's proposal. She could not yet recover from her surprise of what had happened; it was impossible to think of anything else. She had nothing to do to distract her mind, full of thoughts of his insufferable arrogance, and so she decided soon after breakfast to indulge herself in air and exercise.

The morning would have been the perfect combination of warm spring air and blooming flowers—if only the sun had made an appearance. Instead the cloudy sky matched her disturbed mind, and she hoped it would not rain and spoil her walk. In the distance, she discerned some angry thunder-clouds, but they seemed far off. Her steps led her at first to her favourite path, until the recollection that Mr Darcy sometimes walked there led her in a different direction, and instead of entering the park, she turned up the lane which led her farther from the road. The park fence ran along on one side, and soon she passed by one of the gates which led into the grounds.

It was five weeks since she first arrived in Kent, during

which time the trees lost that pale tint of spring and bloomed into the full green of summer. As she approached Rosings Park, she gazed through the gate and down the lane, flooded with bluebells, their vibrant colour a rebellion against the overcast sky.

She hesitated. Elizabeth could not deny her fear of encountering Mr Darcy. She often met him in the park, and it was not unreasonable that he should take a walk that morning as well. Was she to think that every chance encounter had been with the express purpose of meeting her? Her cheeks grew warm to think that it had, but she shook off her misgivings and squared her shoulders as she stepped into the grove. Must every morning walk hereafter be determined by the sentiments of another—one whose actions were so wholly disconnected from the feelings of others? Oh no! She would not be intimidated. Indeed, even if Mr Darcy were to walk here, what purpose could he have in mind? There could be no question of her sentiments; she felt them as keenly now as she had the previous afternoon.

No sooner had she taken a few paces down the lane than she heard a twig snap ahead and caught a glimpse of a gentleman. In spite of all her resolve, she was about to turn back to the parsonage when she heard her name pronounced, and, before she could leave, Mr Darcy came striding towards her.

He reached her in no time, holding out a letter which she instinctively took. She tipped her head to look at him, noticing that he looked down his nose at her, holding himself straight. The morning breeze picked up and blew his dark hair back, giving her a good look at his eyes. She could not detect either remorse or anger there and felt some relief that he seemed to be as haughtily composed as usual.

"I have been walking the grove some time in the hope of meeting you. Will you do me the honour of reading this letter?" With a slight bow, he turned and was soon out of sight.

The wind now whipping her skirt about, she heard a thunderclap overhead. The rainclouds, so far away moments ago, were covering the sun. She looked down at the letter in her hand, Mr Darcy's insulting proposal ringing in her ears.

"Could you expect me to rejoice in the inferiority of your connexions?—to congratulate myself on the hope of relations, whose condition in life is so decidedly beneath my own?"

What could he mean by writing a letter to her? The thunder above threatened again, but the blood was pounding in her ears and she only had eyes for the letter. What could he mean by it? Without any expectation of pleasure, but with the strongest curiosity, her hands began to break the seal. As it opened, the envelope tore with a delicious rip, and the first two pages of the letter with it.

Elizabeth let out a gasp that turned into a laugh. She felt a rush of liberation, all of the anger she felt yesterday afternoon coursing through her. Without thinking of the consequences, she pulled forcefully and the letter was in two. Placing one page on top of the other, she pulled again, the letter shredding with a satisfying swish. Mr Darcy could not have anything worthy to say. Did he think that an apology was within his power?

After all that he had done to cause unhappiness in the lives of so many—to approach her with a letter! What could he mean by it? Knowing enough of Mr Darcy's pride, it could not be a renewal of his addresses. What then had he wished to address? A defence of his character? Every proud word, every insult to her family, every injustice committed against Jane and Mr Wickham flooded her mind and into the force of her hands as she tore the remaining pages and let them fall to the grass.

At that moment, heavy raindrops started coming down, and the thunder crashed again, shocking her into awareness of the moment. She found herself staring at the letter on the ground as the raindrops stained the very close hand.

With a pang, she knelt down to retrieve the letter, the ink now running and the letters illegible. What had she done? She held in her hand an explanation, and although she was certain that it could have no bearing on *any* of her feelings, she had destroyed what had perhaps been the careful work of many hours in a moment of anger.

He had been in love with her for so many months, so much so that he had wished to marry her in spite of those objections which had caused him to separate Bingley from her sister. A reply to her accusations against him with regard to Jane or Mr Wickham? Could he attempt to deny his cruelty towards that gentleman?

Elizabeth's spirits were vexed at this thought. How could Mr Darcy put her in this position? Imagine, writing a letter!

By this time her dress was becoming soaked and she knew that she must hasten back to the parsonage. Looking down at the ruined letter, she folded it up as best she could, putting it into her pocket.

In the steady rain she ran back to parsonage, going around the back to slip into the house. Her thoughts were now as discomposed as her appearance—and she had no desire to be seen in such a state. She crept up the stairs to her room, closing the door. Stripping off her wet garments, she donned a new dress and dried her hair by the fire.

Recalling Mr Darcy's letter, she pulled it out of her wet dress pocket, now soaked through. To have it tear quite unintentionally at the first—but with what subsequent joy had she destroyed it afterwards! Feeling some remorse, she peeled back the paper she had folded together to find that the water had melted the words away so that only a blur remained. She sighed, rubbing her temples as the headache from yesterday started to return. The only point upon which she did not look with regret was her refusal of Mr Darcy. At least in *that*, there had been no mistake.

It was an hour before she felt presentable enough—her composure intact, and her hair completely dry—to descend downstairs and face Charlotte's astute gaze. She found Maria and Charlotte in the parlour.

Maria leapt up. "Oh Lizzy, we thought you were caught in the rain!"

"I was! Indeed, I sneaked back into the house to avoid detection, such was the state of my appearance!" Elizabeth took Charlotte's offered cup of tea.

"Mr Darcy has sent a note, Elizabeth," Charlotte said once Elizabeth was settled into a chair.

Elizabeth coughed, having choked a little on her tea. "A note?"

"With his and Colonel Fitzwilliam's compliments," she replied. "They had planned to take their leave in person, but the weather put paid to all their best intentions."

"Indeed?" Elizabeth sipped her tea to hide her expression. What a relief he had not come! One meeting in the park was enough for a single morning.

"What a shame that the Colonel did not come—such a handsome gentleman! I am sure he could sweep you off your feet!" Maria fanned herself with a napkin in a mock swoon.

"Maria!" Charlotte narrowed her eyes.

"I am sure Colonel Fitzwilliam could charm many a woman, but he is no object of mine." Elizabeth's reply surprised even herself. "I am not sorry to see either of them go."

"Well, I shall be very sorry to see you both go." Charlotte poured them more tea. "Can you not be prevailed upon to stay longer? Lady Catherine herself has condescended to say that you would be welcome for another month complete. My dear husband is determined that you will be spared no comfort. And truly, I have grown quite dependent on your company."

Elizabeth smiled and reached over to take her friend's hand. "You know how much affection I hold for you, but I must rejoin Jane."

Charlotte sighed, "I cannot blame you. What laments we will hear from Lady Catherine to lose all of her company nearly at once!"

With a thrill, Elizabeth wondered what that Lady would have thought if, today, instead of making his departure, Mr Darcy had presented her to Lady Catherine as her future *niece*. She shook her head, marveling at the idea of such a reversal of fortune. It would not do to think of such things.

The remaining days at Hunsford passed quickly and uneventfully. Elizabeth had a disposition that was not given to ill humour, and whatever unpleasant feelings might have arisen at the thought of Mr Darcy's unfortunate letter were soon overcome. She was not certain what to do with the now-dried but smudged paper until at last she decided that it was best to burn it. As she watched the flames consume his work, she resolved not to think on it; she hoped that soon enough she need never think of him again.

NOT THINKING OF MR DARCY, HOWEVER, WAS EASIER SAID than done. From Hunsford, she and Maria set out to London, where they would rejoin Jane for two weeks before returning to Hertfordshire. And with each mile of distance between them and Hunsford, Elizabeth could not help but recall Mr Bingley's lack of resolve in matters of the heart. How would she tell Jane that there was no hope? That, indeed, *Mr Darcy* was the agent of her misery and separation from the one she loved? It was impossible!

Upon their arrival in London, Elizabeth found Jane

looking better than she expected. It was with joy that she was reunited with both Jane and her aunt and uncle. She knew that she owed her aunt a debt of gratitude for keeping up Jane's spirits.

Indeed, the Gardiner home was filled to the brim with engagements and activities and eager young children, so much so that Elizabeth never found a moment to speak to Jane alone. Elizabeth understood the information she had to relay would greatly astonish Jane, but it was easier to keep the news of Mr Darcy's proposal and letter to herself. Longbourn—and the comfort of home—would give her the opportunity to share her news and feelings adequately.

On the road from London to Longbourn, it was with surprise that they found themselves met at the appointed inn by Kitty and Lydia, who came in their father's carriage to meet them.

Lydia was most triumphant as she led them upstairs to a private room in the inn, where a large assortment of cold foods was laid out on the table. "Look, is this not nice?" she cried. "We have here the most delicious assortment of foods imaginable—but oh, Jane! You will have to lend us your money to pay for it, because I have spent all my money in the shop."

"Lydia has bought herself a revolting piece of work," Kitty giggled as they sat and began to eat.

"I might as well have bought it as not, and you will see how becoming it will be when I have pulled it to pieces at home." Lydia brandished an offensive bonnet and both Jane and Lizzy obliged her by abusing it for some moments as exceedingly ugly.

"It is not as if it matters what anyone wears anymore this summer—" Kitty began.

"—for the militia are to leave Meryton and will be encamped at Brighton for the whole summer," pouted Lydia.

"They are leaving in a fortnight," Kitty said with an aggrieved sigh.

"Indeed?" Elizabeth frowned as she thought of the last time she spoke of Mr Wickham, and how Mr Darcy's face had flushed when she mentioned his accusations.

"I have no opinion on the subject whatsoever," Jane announced. "The status of the militia does not concern me one way or the other."

"Perhaps it should concern you, and you should not be so unaffected." Lydia leaned closer, "I am sure we could find you the perfect match and in a beautiful red coat. And Lizzy, you could show more interest since *you* like a certain person nearly as much as the rest of us! Look, she will try to deny it!"

Maria, enjoying the laughter of Kitty and Lydia, joined in as Elizabeth said curtly that she did not.

"Oh, Lizzy, you should not be so cross all the time. You have not even heard our plan!" Kitty said.

"Yes, and it is a good deal merrier than anything we have thought of yet! Why not have Papa take us all to Brighton for the summer? I daresay there would be little expense—" Lydia paused to take a breath.

"—and it would be such a delightful scheme. We have persuaded Mama and she would like to go now above all things!" Kitty finished.

Lydia snorted and turned with a conspiratorial look to Maria. "Kitty neglects the *most* delicious part," she nodded towards Elizabeth. "It is excellent news, most capital, and about that very *certain* person we all like!"

Jane and Elizabeth looked at each other and informed the waiter that he need not stay.

"That is so like you, all discretion and formality," Lydia laughed, "as if the ugly fellow had heard nothing worse in his whole life! What a long face. He looked like a horse. Well, but now for my news: it is about dear Wickham. He is safe! There is no danger at all of him marrying Mary King after all, and she has gone to stay with her uncle in Liverpool for good. There's for you!"

This surprised Elizabeth. "Oh! I thought the attachment between them was stronger."

Lydia was sufficiently gratified, waggling her eyebrows at Maria and Kitty. "There, I knew she would like our news!"

"I do *hope* there was no strong attachment on either side," Jane began, but Lydia interrupted.

"I should say not, for such a nasty little freckled thing!"

Elizabeth almost laughed at the description, for it was one which she had often thought of herself, but checked her impulse when she remembered Jane's concern.

"I am sure he never cared two straws about her," Kitty asserted.

The ladies finished their repast and set out towards Longbourn. The rest of the journey was passed in the most cramped situation possible. Lydia was not content during the entire drive to do anything but complain of the bags—which she insisted should remain in the carriage—and talked of otherwise everything and nothing. Elizabeth was granted a headache, but it was lifted at the sight of Longbourn.

Mrs Bennet was very happy to find her daughters in good health, and Jane in such undiminished beauty. Their father seemed more delighted than usual, and several times during dinner voluntarily said, "I am glad you are come back, Lizzy."

After dinner, Lydia suggested they walk to Meryton. Although she was tempted by the idea of once again seeing the newly unattached Mr Wickham, Elizabeth did not approve of her sister's need to spend the earliest moment possible in pursuit of soldiers. That suggestion was therefore given up until another day.

The talk of Brighton, however, was not so easily given up. As the evening went on, Elizabeth was impressed by the frequency and energy with which her youngest sisters and her mother brought up their scheme of a summer in Brighton. Her father, she noted, had not said no, but did not seem in any humour to oblige them.

Her first response was relief that her two younger sisters would not parade about with red coats for the world to see. But then again, why shouldn't they enjoy themselves, under the guidance of herself and Jane, perhaps? They had never been to the sea. Brighton's social attractions did not hold the interest for her that it did for her youngest sisters, but she heard that the beauty of the nearby landscape in Sussex was unparalleled. From Brighton, they might even see other wonders. Perhaps the scheme was not so bad, after all, with a little encouragement in the right direction.

THE SCHEME THAT WAS BRIGHTON

*N*ow that they were home, Elizabeth was bursting to tell Jane the news of what had happened between herself and Mr Darcy.

The opportunity afforded itself the morning after their arrival, when Elizabeth decided to pull Jane alone with her down the lane and into a bit of wilderness on the far side of the park.

"Jane, I must—" She took off her bonnet and twisted it in her hands before continuing to speak. "There is something important I have been meaning to tell you and I have not had the opportunity. I was—that is, indeed, this is vexing! You will think me a fool!"

"Tsk, Lizzy, never! It is not like you to keep secrets. Tell me and be done with it."

And then the words tumbled forward in a great rush. "You know I mentioned that Mr Darcy came to Hunsford, and with him his cousin, Colonel Fitzwilliam. But what I did not mention was that Mr Darcy often met me unexpectedly in the park. I would walk alone, as usual, and he would happen upon me and walk with me a long way and ask me questions about whether I liked living in the country, and whether I should always like to be so near Longbourn and it all was so perplexing—until the evening of his proposal to me."

Jane gasped and took her hand.

"He came to call at Hunsford and I did not know what to think except that he wanted to criticise, but then he declared his feelings for me—" Elizabeth paused, remembering his expression when he said that his feelings could not be overcome, "and in such an arrogant and conceited way that...He expected my acceptance—that it would be such an honour for me to receive an offer of marriage from him that I could not dare refuse it. He made his feelings about my station *perfectly* clear. I was obliged not only to refuse him, but to tell him in no uncertain terms that he was the last man in the world whom I could ever marry."

Jane's eyes widened. "Lizzy, I am amazed! I cannot think that—but of course it is no surprise to me that he should be in love with you!"

Elizabeth let out a laugh, "You would not be surprised to find out that anyone was in love with me. That is your nature!"

"Truly, Lizzy, how unfortunate for Mr Darcy. It was wrong of him to be so certain of his acceptance. It must increase his disappointment all the more."

"Certainly he has other feelings, so well expressed, that will soon drive away his regard for me." Elizabeth shook her shoulders as if to brush off the memory of his disdain for her family connexions. "You do not blame me, however, for refusing him?"

"Blame you, oh no!"

"But you will blame me when you hear what must follow, for indeed I have felt moments of shame myself. He wrote me a letter."

"A letter! To what purpose? Was he able to defend himself

in any respect?" Jane did not attempt to conceal her eagerness to discover its contents.

"Jane, I—do not know. I no longer have the letter in my possession, and have never read it at all."

"How—"

"It tore, Jane, when I first began to open it, and I could not prevent it."

"Of course you could not prevent a tear—but that does not ruin a letter." Jane seemed at a loss.

"I felt such release at finishing the work that I accidentally began. I destroyed the letter, everything torn to pieces, and at that very moment it began to rain! He wrote with such a close hand—the water made short work of any remaining words."

Jane was silent at first. "I do not know what to say," she began.

"Jane, please. I know that he could not have renewed his addresses to me; that was made clear. Nothing he might have said would have—could have—changed my opinion." Elizabeth began to feel distressed as Jane's pain for Mr Darcy, undeserving man as he was, became more and more evident.

Jane moved away from her sister to sit under the shade of an oak. "Lizzy, it was wrong of you to destroy Mr Darcy's letter."

Elizabeth moved to sit next to her on the grass, feeling warmth spread from her neck to her cheeks. Remorse came flooding forward and caught in her throat. "I am sorry, Jane. I tore it to shreds before I even realised; I allowed myself to be ruled by indignation."

"You had a right to feel indignant."

"His manner of address, his pride! Furthermore, what if it became known that I received a private communication from him?"

"That he took such a chance can only mean that what he

wished to say to you was very important," said Jane, with too much reason for Elizabeth to like.

"At least he will never know that you destroyed it. Perhaps the letter would have caused you pain, for I am sure it must have been written with great bitterness of spirit," Jane continued, and then attempted to smile.

"I would wish never to set eyes on him again. And for your sake alone, Jane, do I fervently hope that his pain will be short lived. I do not desire to cause pain to anyone—but I am certain his will be of short duration. You must be wrong. He could not have been in love with me. Indeed, how could such a man with so little regard for the feelings of others? Have you forgotten his treatment of Wickham?" Elizabeth herself had not thought of Wickham since the day Lydia mentioned Brighton.

"You may be right; it is distressing. What can one think in such a situation?"

"You will have to allow me to be in the right." Elizabeth ducked away from her sister's gentle swat. "Allow me to be right that Mr Darcy's feelings are no great loss. We are not likely to see him again."

Jane's eyes flashed with sadness at this sentiment, but she then shrugged her shoulders with resolve. "I will forgive you for tearing Mr Darcy's letter if you will agree to feel a bit sorry for him. He does not seem like the sort of man who would forget easily. He was not always so easy in company as you. To propose! In spite of our connexions! I know what it is to have felt—in any case, I will forgive you if you promise to help me to forget my own troubles."

"You must not be unhappy, dearest." Elizabeth moved to hold her close. "Mr Bingley was not worthy of you! Any man who does not see what you are is not."

"That is absurd, Lizzy," Jane said, moving away. "Mr Bingley is above reproach. He did not promise me anything.

And I was spared the pain of an embarrassing encounter over the winter. I will be happy, again, you will see!"

"I will see *to* it," Elizabeth replied, and helped her up to walk back into the house.

ELIZABETH HAD NOT TAKEN TWO STEPS FORWARD DOWN THE hall towards the library when round the corner she nearly collided with her mother lying in wait.

"Now you see, Lizzy," Mrs Bennet lamented as she grabbed hold of Elizabeth's arm and turned her towards the sitting room, "this sad business of Jane's. I told my sister Philips just the other day that I am determined not to speak of it any longer. Such an undeserving young man—and I cannot find out anything of his coming back to Netherfield! I have asked anyone who would have heard anything."

"I do not believe that he will ever live at Netherfield anymore, Mama."

"I suppose it makes no difference to us. Though I shall always say that he used my daughter extremely ill! If I were her, I should never have put up with it. My comfort is that Jane will die of a broken heart, and then he will be sorry."

Elizabeth did not find such thoughts comforting in the least so did not reply.

"I know that the Collinses are living quite comfortably—I am sure they work with a great deal of management. They will never outrun their income! And I suppose they often talk of it. I am sure they discuss it frequently between themselves. So much the better if they can be easy with an estate that is not lawfully their own, but *I* should be ashamed of having one that was only entailed on me!"

To this Elizabeth could offer no comment. Mrs Bennet had a long history of refusing to comprehend the truth of an entail.

Mrs Bennet went on to describe to Elizabeth in great detail

her plan for their stay in Brighton. She was persuaded that if Elizabeth would agree to the scheme, then Mr Bennet would do so as well. Elizabeth listened with conflicting feelings; she had intended to travel that summer to the Lakes with her aunt and uncle Gardiner and had been looking forward to their journey for quite some time. To go to Brighton would mean she had to abandon that scheme.

But the state of Jane's distress affected her, as did even their mother's unhappiness, and it made her feel reluctant to leave them. A notion began to form, and to her amazement it was in agreement with Mrs Bennet's plans. Would it not be beneficial if the whole family were to take a trip to Brighton? The city was magnificent and entertaining to say the least, and with the family present, they could perhaps keep Lydia and Kitty in check.

Elizabeth at first said nothing to her mother, but put the idea before Jane. Jane was surprised at first by Lizzy's agreement with the plan, but it did not take much persuasion before she began to see the benefits. Her eyes seemed to display some joy at the thought of such distraction, but she was distressed at the idea of missing the opportunity to visit her young cousins, who were to stay at Longbourn while their parents and Elizabeth toured the Lakes. It was here that Elizabeth revealed something more: their aunt and uncle, along with their cousins, should join them at the seaside. This change moved the plan from general scheme to Grand Scheme. Jane was delighted.

"Lizzy!" she exclaimed, "I am happily remembered of an acquaintance I resumed during my stay in London. On more than one occasion we met Mr and Mrs Bartell, who are distant cousins. Indeed, their grandmother is our great-aunt, the old Mrs Bartell, who is a widow but refuses to leave her house in Brighton. They often mentioned it, worrying over her health. Their unmarried sister is her companion, and she can rarely leave her grandmother. They spoke of her need for a holiday."

"Have we met the old Mrs Bartell?"

"As children, I believe. I do not remember the particulars, but she is now infirm and requires care. She has not travelled from Brighton in some years. I will write to Mr and Mrs Bartell and enquire—perhaps we could stay with old Mrs Bartell and relieve her granddaughter for the summer!"

Jane sent out her correspondence that very afternoon, and did not have to wait long for a reply. Miss Bartell would be eternally grateful for a summer holiday—she had family to visit in the North, and Mrs Bartell herself would welcome the Bennet family with open arms.

Every morning at breakfast, the family could not even butter their toast before the subject of Brighton and officers was brought forth, lamented, pleaded, and fretted over in turn by Lydia, Kitty, and lastly Mrs Bennet.

Mr Bennet listened to these sentiments with a mixture of mirth and indifference, and appeared subsequently astonished to hear Elizabeth address him so: "Papa, perhaps it would be a good thing if we did all go to Brighton."

So amazed by the application was he that Mr Bennet, in fact, dropped his toast. "Lizzy, *you* wish to go to Brighton? Whatever put this notion into your head?"

"It is not only Lizzy, Papa," Jane said, "we have all been convinced of its merits. And Lizzy has brought forth the proposition that Aunt and Uncle Gardiner, instead of touring the Lakes, could come with us to the seashore! Thus keeping us in Lizzy's dear company, and adding to the party on the whole."

"We have a relation in common with the Gardiners in Brighton—the Widow Bartell," Elizabeth went on. Their father's amazement was overcome by his amusement.

"Mrs Bartell is in need of a companion for the summer.

Our scheme could thus be accomplished with very little expense to the whole family," Jane continued.

The exaltation that Mrs Bennet felt to have her two oldest daughters so unexpectedly side with her knew no bounds. She was beyond words.

Lydia, however, was not. She immediately began, along with Kitty, to expound upon the joys which they were so soon to experience. Mr Bennet could not respond to such raptures, and Elizabeth noticed his withdrawal. She and Jane worked to silence their youngest sisters, allowing the family to eat in relative silence.

Mr Bennet withheld his judgment for as long as he could bear to keep Jane and Elizabeth in suspense, nearly a quarter of an hour, at the end of which he rose from the table and announced, "It seems that since I am quite outnumbered, and, I must say, overruled on the matter, we have no choice but to take ourselves to the sea. What we will do there I cannot begin to imagine. I will put the idea forth to my brother-in-law." Following this pronouncement, he disappeared into his study.

In the imagination of Kitty and Lydia, Brighton comprised every possibility of earthly happiness. Their exuberance could not be repressed, despite Jane and Elizabeth's best attempts. Their rapture was so complete, that for a moment Elizabeth began to doubt her reason—for what possible good could come of such a display of frivolity?

It was with regret that she recalled Mr Darcy's advice to Mr Bingley on account of there being objections to the lady. Could the behaviour of her youngest sisters have been the cause of those objections? She did not dwell on such thoughts for long and felt disappointed that it seemed she could not put his proposal completely from her mind.

ELIZABETH WAS NOT THE SORT TO REMAIN OUT OF SPIRITS, AND her natural happy disposition, in addition to the Grand Brighton Scheme, as she thought of it, soon helped to brighten Jane's mood. It was not long before they walked together with their younger sisters as a merry party to tell anyone they encountered along the way that they were to go to the sea.

It was with pleasure that one of the first persons they happened to encounter on the road to Meryton was Mr Wickham.

Elizabeth was struck by how agreeable and easy his manners were—how different he was from Mr Darcy! How warm and open his smile was! She recalled his interest in freckled little Miss King, and almost laughed aloud when she recalled her aunt's warning against him.

"You are amused, Miss Bennet, which does not surprise me in the least. I have longed for your company."

"You, I think, have had much better company than mine these last few months," Elizabeth found herself replying with a sly gaze. But, she thought herself not in any danger.

"Alas, you wound me when I, as yet, am not healed," Wickham clasped his hands to his heart and staggered back for a moment as if in agony.

"I can leave you, if you like, to bemoan the loss of better companions," Elizabeth laughed.

"Leave me and my heart will burst anew," Mr Wickham's eyes seemed unusually bright, and Elizabeth wondered if he did feel the loss. It seemed that no one's heart escaped the pierce of Cupid's arrow over the spring.

"I could regale you with tales of the rector of Hunsford— indeed the most interesting man in Kent—but I fear you already know enough of that man and that family with whom he is most ingratiatingly connected."

Mr Wickham turned his head with interest at this. "Why

yes, the journey into Kent! You must tell me, Miss Elizabeth, was the fireplace at Rosings *everything* you wished it to be?"

"Indeed, Mr Wickham, I could not have asked for a more wonderful spectacle. Did you know that we dined at Rosings several times? I daresay Lady Catherine de Bourgh could not have condescended any lower."

"What *did* you think of the daughter?"

"Oh, a better suited pair I have never met than Miss de Bourgh and her intended husband. His haughty demeanour is paired ideally with her silent crossness!" Elizabeth laughed, "We met with him, you know, at Rosings, along with his cousin, Colonel Fitzwilliam. Are you acquainted with the Colonel?"

Wickham's laughter ceased, "Colonel Fitzwilliam? And Darcy? Did you say you saw Darcy? You met with them often?"

"Oh yes," Elizabeth leaned forward conspiratorially, "We were forced to enjoy their company for nearly three weeks. Mr Darcy called often. But Colonel Fitzwilliam is—"

"His manners," Wickham interrupted, "are very different from his cousin's."

"Yes, I liked him very much."

"But I hope your opinion of Mr Darcy has remained unchanged?"

Elizabeth tilted her head with curiosity. "Why should it change?" She remembered Mr Darcy's face when she had mentioned Wickham's name.

The moment was broken by Lydia's shrill laughter and quick steps as she moved between them to take Wickham's arm. He turned so as to speak directly to Elizabeth with a knowing glance towards her sister. "You will forgive my impertinence, Miss Elizabeth. Darcy is in the happy position to please where he chooses—and is not very fond of me."

"Mr Darcy!" Lydia exclaimed. "I have not thought of him

since the winter! I should not like to think of such an odious man again for another six-month!"

"We will not speak his name again, then, shall we, Mr Wickham," Elizabeth cried, "and do not think for a moment that such deception could affect me!"

To this the three of them all agreed most heartily, although Mr Wickham could not help but to lament his position and the unfortunate circumstances in which he found himself. Elizabeth wondered if this was because he regretted not just his position but his inability to pay *her* the attention which his heart dearly longed for.

A YOUNG WOMAN STOOD AT THE WINDOW PANE, LOOKING OUT onto the busy London street. The sun beat down on the cobblestones, and she moved away from the window to fan herself. Her brother was reading the paper, and she hesitated before sitting next to him.

"Fitzwilliam," she began, playing with her fan, "after the events of last summer, will you never—" She faltered when he stiffened.

His attention now wholly diverted, he turned towards her even as she avoided his gaze. "You must finish what you have begun, Georgie."

She sighed, "It is too much. I should not ask anything of you, after all."

"I insist. You must ask—you must never be afraid to ask for what you want." He thought of her young heart, so broken last summer. His heart tightened at the thought of his own desire, now impossibly out of reach.

"It is the seaside. I do not wish to return to Ramsgate, but I love the sea. This heat is so unbearable. But I know how you long to go home."

Darcy considered his sister's hands nervously fiddling

with her fan. He moved his own hands to still them and smiled. "Visiting one does not preclude the other. We could visit the sea together—and perhaps our party would enjoy the trip for a week before journeying to Pemberley for the remainder of the summer. A short trip." A trip that would distract his own troubled mind. A trip meant for forgetting before returning to the home where he would be reminded at every turn what he lost due to his own pride.

Georgiana's hands flew around his neck. "Thank you," she breathed, "you are too kind to me."

ST JAMES'S PLACE

*W*ith exceedingly great raptures the Gardiners' note was received accepting the change in plan from the Lake tour to the Brighton seaside. The Gardiners were delighted by the idea of a visit that included the entire family and noted that Brighton was close to the Seven Sisters chalk cliffs, which they longed to see. The only difficulty was that they must postpone their journey by two weeks because of Mr Gardiner's business. This threw Kitty and Lydia into a flutter of nerves over the thought of even the briefest separation from the officers, until it was decided that the Bennets would travel ahead to Brighton and, within a short amount of time, be joined by the rest of their party.

Elizabeth briefly doubted her impulse to travel with her family during the chaos of packing trunks and gowns and hats and trims with two younger sisters who fought over every item of clothing. At last, once the coach was loaded, the journey was spent in the highest of spirits and Elizabeth felt her doubts give way to eager anticipation.

Even Mary, who never before expressed approval of the scheme and mostly observed her youngest sisters' antics with a frown, now turned to her oldest sisters with a smile. "I have been reading about the benefits of sea bathing," she pronounced, "and the sea itself seems to be a great testament to the power of a great God. I do not care for the parties or the dresses, but I do look forward to seeing this wonder."

"So *you* are to go sea bathing?" Mr Bennet asked with a wry grin. "Do wonders never cease? I surmise that these new environs will provide opportunities for laughter at other people's expense in every corner."

After a stop in London, where the Bennets spent a merry evening with the Gardiners in high anticipation of them all being together again as soon as Mr Gardiner's business was concluded, the second leg of their journey was more subdued, with nearly all of the party sleeping along the road.

It was evening when the Bennets arrived at the home of their relation. The young ladies were all abuzz when the coach stopped on St James's Street, and Mr Bennet led them through a narrow alley and back to a quiet lane, known as St James's Place, where a row of town houses and gardens stood. The four-story red brick town house where they would spend their holiday had a small garden full of roses enclosed by an iron railing.

"How charming! And you cannot hear the noise of the street!" Elizabeth said.

"But my dear you did not tell me that Mrs Bartell lived so close to the shops! So close to everything! Why, what a thing for our girls! I am sure they shall always be thrown in the path of many eligible men. I can hardly speak for happiness." Mrs Bennet's mouth was agape at the sight of the stately home.

"You need not speak at all," Mr Bennet replied. "I would not put much hope in Mrs Bartell's potential as a matchmaker."

"Why ever not?" Mrs Bennet said, but Mr Bennet had already opened the gate and walked up the steps to rap on the door. Behind him, the coachmen were huffing as they carried the many trunks.

The door was opened by a woman much advanced in years who led them through a narrow hall into a sitting room where another woman even more advanced in years sat dozing in a blue velvet chair.

The attendant, a Mrs Smith, shook the shoulder of her employer with some vigour. She managed to knock the lady's cap askew but did not wake her.

With all of them crowding the hall, and the trunks piling up along the wall, there was a moment of tension as they were not entirely sure what to do next. It was relieved by Mrs Bennet, who marched up to their relation and shouted into her ear, "It is so very kind of you to allow us to stay!"

Mrs Bartell opened one eye and shifted slightly. "You are looking old, Mrs B," she croaked.

Mrs Bennet was so offended that she moved off immediately, whispering to Elizabeth, "She is farther gone than I imagined. Pay no mind to her ramblings. Indeed, I have half a mind not to speak with her much at all—I daresay she cannot understand a word."

Elizabeth did not rebuke her mother, but moved over to Mrs Bartell. "And you, madam," she laughed, "do not look a day over twenty!"

Mrs Bartell deigned to open both eyes. "Tom Bennet, this one will do nicely," she declared, reaching to take Elizabeth's hand. "You will have to oblige me. My granddaughter has left this morning for the North, and I need looking after. It is part of the arrangement."

"Lizzy is always very obliging." Mrs Bennet felt that she must speak again. "We are so very grateful for the most warm welcome into your home."

"*And* will you oblige me now by removing all of your relations from my sitting room." Mrs Bartell addressed Elizabeth, "Your rooms are on the third floor."

Kitty and Lydia scampered from the room and up the stairs, with the older sisters following closely. While the others settled their trunks into their rooms, Elizabeth moved through the entire house, curious to see each room and the views they afforded. Upon returning to the blue room that she and Jane had settled on with Mary, Elizabeth flung open the tall windows to breathe in the salty air of the sea. The lights of the city twinkled before her, but in spite of the pleadings of Lydia, who wanted to go and tour the public gardens (where she was certain the officers were waiting), it was decided that the party would go to bed and explore in the morning.

ELIZABETH ROSE AT HER CUSTOMARY HOUR AND WALKED downstairs to find Mrs Bartell with Mrs Smith eating a hearty breakfast.

"You must join me, Miss Elizabeth," she said and gestured towards the cut of cold ham. You look as though you could do with some fattening up."

"I thank you, Mrs Bartell, but I will wait until after my walk. The sea calls."

"Then you must answer, but you are required to return within the hour and I will join you. Will your sisters be up?"

"They do not keep early hours," Elizabeth said.

"And neither does Mrs B?" Seeing Elizabeth's smirk, she continued "Ah, well, I see then that your mother is the most fashionable of them all. I cannot abide by fashion. When Mr Bartell was alive we never kept such hours. And we never ate such slight things as toast in the morning. No indeed, you must have mutton and ale. Breakfast. You will be required to partake in breakfast."

"After I have seen the sea, I am sure to need sustenance." Elizabeth fastened her bonnet over her dark hair and slipped outdoors.

The early morning of Brighton was not the still and solitary quiet of her usual countryside walks. While the fashionable slept, the fishermen and shipwrights bustled about, and the shopkeepers prepared their wares. She made her way through the busy cobblestone streets and out to the beach, where empty carts lined the rocky beach in anticipation of a rush of guests. These must be the famous bathing machines used by the visitors to partake in the cleansing waters of the English channel.

Elizabeth turned her eyes away from the city and out across the expanse, now shifting from blue to green and back again as the sunlight played across the water. She made her way across the rocks carefully, finding surer footing as the rocks became smaller, finer pebbles closer to the crashing waves. The wind blew teasingly against her face, and the sea stretched before her, limitless and terrifying. The white of the buildings and beach contrasted with the colourful waves, and she could almost taste the salt as she breathed in deeply. No wonder it was here, at the sea, so wide and wild, that stories were told of the mermaids' siren call, luring men out into the deep.

She took a deep breath and, seeing no one about, stretched her arms wide, turning in a circle with her face towards the sky. This was the moment she had been waiting for. She felt the tension of the past year ease out of her shoulders and realised with some happiness that she had not thought of Mr Darcy or his letter for the whole of two days. She would not need to think of him or Mr Bingley or any other man. What are men to rocks and sea? The roaring of the waves blocked out thoughts of anything else. The bustling city offered a vast array of diversions for Jane. Here was a place they would forget their troubles and be merry.

After some minutes alone, she turned back, finding that, even though the hour drew close to ten, her mother and youngest sisters had not yet stirred from their beds. But Jane was conversing with Mrs Bartell, and her father had already breakfasted.

"Here you are Lizzy," Mary spoke with some eagerness, "I should like to try sea-bathing today."

"You waste no time!" Elizabeth said.

"Nor do you," called Jane. "You've already gone and come back. And how do you like Brighton?"

"Very much indeed."

"We shall have to take you sea bathing as soon as the opportunity affords," Mrs Bartell announced.

"I should like to bathe in the sea—something so open. And I understand that the health benefits are unsurpassed," Elizabeth smiled.

Mrs Bartell took several moments to expound upon the sea's many benefits before Mrs Bennet and the younger girls finally appeared. It was agreed that the whole family would venture out to bathe.

The ladies lost an entire hour at least preparing to go out the door; Lydia and Kitty's searching for the right shoes rivaled the dramatics of a theatrical production, but it was Mrs Bennet who caused the most delay in trying to choose just the right cap. Mrs Bartell could not walk long distances, and her attendant helped Jane and Elizabeth prepare her chair. At first, in the commotion, Mr Bennet disappeared into Mrs Bartell's small reading room, but once the entire party was waiting in the lane, Elizabeth would brook no refusal and Mr Bennet was forced outside.

He was not, however, permitted to remain with the ladies. At the appointed location he ambled off with reluctance but in the certainty of an *experience* to the area where the men were swimming, far from the women.

As the ladies approached the beach, the wind picked up and whipped spray from the sea into the air. A great many seagulls were flocking about, eager to catch a spare morsel from the crowd of visitors. Elizabeth was struck by how different the empty beach was from this midday crush.

Mrs Bennet sputtered against the onslaught. "This weather is dreadful, I do worry about getting into the water."

"Nonsense! There is nothing better for your constitution. It was for this very reason that I came into Brighton some forty years ago when I was *your* age. I take to the water every week," Mrs Bartell insisted.

Mrs Bennet looked out at the stretch of the sea and its lapping waves. "The water is so wild," she whispered to Elizabeth, clenching her arm, "Mrs Bartell does nothing in an ordinary way."

"But all the ladies are sea-bathing!" Lydia said, pulling her mother towards a bathing machine, now operated by a large, athletic woman who called herself a 'dipper'. It was hitched to a horse ready to pull them out a ways into the sea. Jane helped Mrs Bartell get out of her chair to make her way across the beach while the rest clambered into the wooden contraption, one after the other.

Inside, the woman presented them with the choice to strip naked or wear a dark woollen garment. Lydia declared that she would rather swim naked than wear such an odious-coloured cloth, but Mary and Mrs Bennet wavered at the idea of such exposure.

"*I* do not wear the bathing clothes," Mrs Bartell proclaimed, having finally reached the machine, thus settling the question for Mrs Bennet, who decided to change into the bathing costume.

Elizabeth considered the practicality of the matter. "I think that we shall drown in these clothes," she whispered to Jane, who laughed in response even as she struggled into the woolen garment.

"Mrs Forster never mentioned any other ladies bathing with these stupid clothes!"

"Lydia," Elizabeth cried sternly, but the woman attending them assured her that it did not matter one way or the other, and there was no concern for their virtue, as the canopy would shield them from prying eyes. Elizabeth decided to forego the garment, herself, her skin pricking as her foot touched the waves.

Mrs Bennet was terrified. "I cannot do it, I am sure to drown! What would become of you? Look at the sight of the water, it is too deep, I cannot possibly—" But her protests were silenced when the bathing woman promptly plunged her into the water.

Afraid of being so unceremoniously forced in themselves, Jane and Elizabeth slipped in the rest of the way quickly and waded out to sea. Mrs Bartell delighted them by first voluntarily dunking her head under the water and then swimming out away from the canopy and back again.

"I am as light as a feather," she cried, floating on her back.

Elizabeth moved her hands through the cold water, looking down at the murky depths. As her body adjusted to its temperature, she felt a jolt of exhilaration. First she felt the pebbles beneath her feet, pushing herself up and down to bob along with the waves. Then she allowed the buoyancy of the water to hold her aloft, carrying her up and down as if it were breathing.

To her right, she saw Mrs Bartell also floating along, her aged arms gracefully paddling.

"You are a natural, Lizzy," Mrs Bartell called, "Do not be afraid to float out a bit beyond the canopy. Kick your feet!"

Elizabeth experimented with paddling her feet as she bobbed along with the waves, delighted with the propulsion. She was not an experienced swimmer, but she had learned to float in the small pond at Longbourn in her youth. To her left, her sisters remained on shallower ground, and were splashing each other hesitantly and laughing. She turned to face the horizon and looked at the vast expanse of water, longing to swim out farther to the edge of everything, and wondering what strange creatures lurked below the waves.

Feeling a tug at her foot, she gasped and spun about, surprised to find Jane standing behind.

"You!" Elizabeth said, splashing her with water, "You gave me a fright! I imagined for a moment a sea creature dragging me down!"

Jane only laughed and returned the spray of water. Soon a full-blown battle ensued, joined by Kitty and Lydia. Mary was reluctant to fling any water about, but found it amusing when she managed to dunk a wailing Lydia beneath the waves.

The bathing woman did not find their behaviour to her tastes, and so their bath did not last as long as Elizabeth should have liked. Mrs Bennet was only too eager to scramble back into their machine, dripping forlornly, her teeth chattering. "I do not see any p-p-possible benefit from such th-things. The w-water is a great deal too expansive. I must get home, I am fairly—fairly f-faint from exhaustion!" Her laments continued thus as she was supported home by her two eldest daughters, with Mary following primly to help Mrs Bartell, and Kitty and Lydia giggling all the way.

MRS BENNET'S NERVES WERE SUFFICIENTLY RATTLED THAT SHE remained in her chambers the whole of the afternoon, and could only be persuaded from her room that evening to walk out to see the fireworks along the gardens at the insistence of Lydia, who was keen to seek out the militia quartered at Brighton.

The fashionable society of Brighton was now out and about, and the streets were illuminated even through the night. Mrs Bennet was acquainted well enough with society's customs to know that one way to catch a husband was to walk and take tea in the gardens, so she made herself available as a chaperone while Kitty and Lydia were let loose on the sea of officers in the gardens.

Elizabeth and Jane found themselves busy keeping the younger girls in check as they were introduced to one red-coat gallant after another, but soon enough they came across their former acquaintances, the Colonel and Mrs Forster, who drank tea with them for a merry hour and insisted that the next day they must visit the circulating library so as to become acquainted with the rest of society.

It was at this moment that a tall, familiar figure spoke from behind them, "Oh, but they cannot give their names at the circulating library, or we shall never be privileged to be in their company again! The Bennet sisters are such beauties that their gifts will be known all over town and they shan't give the time of day to soldiers like us, eh, Denny?"

Lydia squealed with delight, "Oh, Wickham, you gave me such a fright! And to think I despaired of seeing you all! I looked all over the shore today with no luck at all."

"I am delighted that you have found us—but where else should we be than here, in the gardens, drinking of beauty and fireworks?" Wickham smiled at Lydia but turned his gaze to Elizabeth. "And how do you like the sea, Miss Elizabeth?"

"I like it very well indeed, Mr Wickham. Does the bustle of the city suit you?"

"The present company suits me." He offered her his arm as

the whole party paused in their conversation to admire the flaming colours of the fireworks display.

Lydia's smile turned into a pout, and she reached for Mr Wickham's other arm. Mr Wickham thus distracted, Elizabeth turned to look at Jane's face, lit up by the many different colours of the fireworks display. Though surrounded by men, she was alone. If not for Mr Darcy and his interference! How completely had he shattered the hopes and dreams of the present company. Her grasp tightened on Mr Wickham's arm, and he turned to smile at her again.

"LIZZY," BEGAN JANE LATE IN THE NIGHT AFTER THEY returned home and everyone was asleep, "you seem to be taken with Mr Wickham. Yet, I thought…"

Elizabeth wrapped her arms around herself. "I was perfectly resigned to never seeing him as anything but a happy acquaintance. Now I do not know. He is so amiable—"

"And all that is charming," said Jane with a smile. "I cannot help but wonder…"

"It is not like you to wonder at anyone."

Jane blushed. "I am sorry, Lizzy, but do take care. Your life would not be so comfortable as the one you are accustomed to. But, if you truly love each other—"

"Jane! I like him very much, but love?" Elizabeth sighed. "If only Mr Darcy had not brought him so low!"

There was a moment of silence. "Do you think about his letter, still? I wonder—"

"More wondering?" Elizabeth chided gently. She felt her throat clench with a mixture of guilt and curiosity, but she could do nothing to resurrect the letter. "Perhaps I should not have told you, since I cannot change the past or what I have done. We are not likely to see him again, and even so I could never ask him what was in the letter."

"You are right. We will not see them again, will we?"

"There are plenty of other men to divert you here," Elizabeth said, taking her hand.

"Yes, Mama," Jane laughed, and Elizabeth pretended to be offended, so they finally went to bed.

THE CLERGYMAN AND THE OFFICER

*T*he morning found Mrs Bennet with a miserable stuffy nose, but she would not be deterred from rising early to go with Jane to the circulating library in hopes of throwing all five daughters in the path of eligible men.

"Will you not go with us, Mrs Bartell?" she asked with a simultaneous and uproarious sneeze.

"I make it a point never to move in society," Mrs Bartell said, "and you, perhaps, should take yourself to the bathing machine to remedy your cold."

"There is a ball at the Crown Inn this Saturday, and I shall do everything in my power to ensure that my daughters attend." Mrs Bennet sneezed again.

"You are not fit to be seen by anybody," Mrs Bartell sniffed. "Elizabeth, you will take me to church."

"St Nicholas Church?" Mr Bennet enquired.

"The same."

"There's a point of interest for you Lizzy—it was built in the 13th century. You must go and give me a full report."

"Will you not join us Papa? Or perhaps Mary would like to come?"

"Mary is in bed ill," Jane said, "and Kitty and Lydia are still sleeping."

"Yesterday's exertion was enough for a week," Mr Bennet pronounced and moved to settle into an armchair by the window with a book.

It was a long walk to the church, but Elizabeth did not mind. She took turns with Mrs Smith navigating Mrs Bartell's chair over the cobblestone street. Mrs Bartell knew a great deal about the city and passed the journey naming houses and describing when they were erected. Brighton was constantly being built up, but the sight of the medieval church with its Norman-era tower reminded Elizabeth that it had seen visitors come and go for centuries.

The stone church was surrounded by a lawn with a large graveyard, and, after taking a tour inside, Elizabeth took Mrs Bartell to walk amongst the gravestones. The older lady insisted that she wanted to stretch her legs and seemed to enjoy strolling about holding onto Elizabeth's arm.

It caused nothing short of a commotion when she fainted. One moment she was naming some of her former acquaintances, and the next she went heavy on Elizabeth's arm and, before Elizabeth could stop it, slipped down onto the grass. Elizabeth was grateful she was able, at the least, to prevent her from striking her head against one of the stones.

"Mrs Bartell!" she cried out, and Mrs Smith, who had wandered to the other side of the lawn, rushed back. "Mrs Smith, does she often faint?"

"May I be of assistance?" said a voice at her elbow, and Elizabeth turned to see a young man on his knees next to her. "Is Mrs Bartell breathing?"

Elizabeth checked her pulse and nodded in the affirmative.

"Oh, Mr Walker, how glad I am to see you here! Help us

take her back to her chair!" Mrs Smith said, wringing her hands.

The reverend lifted Mrs Bartell and gently moved her to the wooden chair, and Elizabeth thought she saw the older lady peeking out from one eye.

"Are you awake now, Mrs Bartell?" Elizabeth asked, as Mrs Smith pressed a phial of salts into her hand. "You have given us all a fright!" Upon receiving no response, she moved the salts beneath Mrs Bartell's nose, but the older woman swatted away her hand.

"Good heavens child, I am perfectly well."

"Indeed not," Elizabeth protested, "for you have had a fall."

"I never fall. You are quite mistaken."

"Madam, the lady speaks truth, for you were walking along the gravestones when you swooned and fell to the ground," the young man said.

"Oh, Mr Walker!" Mrs Bartell exclaimed, disregarding all suggestion of her malady. "Have you met my great-niece, Miss Elizabeth Bennet?"

The rector's mouth twitched as if holding back a laugh, and his eyes met Elizabeth's. He inclined his head politely before turning back to Mrs Bartell.

Elizabeth's eyes narrowed in suspicion. Had Mrs Bartell actually fainted, or was this a scheme to involve the young gentleman? As if Elizabeth did not already have enough interference from her own mother! "I think it is time we went home," she announced.

"But you have only just made Mr Walker's acquaintance, and I should like him to give us a tour of the sanctuary."

"If I may insist, mistress, we must go home! You have given us all such a fright!" Mrs Smith proclaimed, taking the smelling salts back from Elizabeth and wiping a tear from her eye.

"Nonsense. I shall not have a lovely morning spoiled. I am capable of being pushed about in my chair."

"Really, Mrs Bartell—" both Mr Walker and Elizabeth spoke at the same time and flushed simultaneously.

"We shall take a tour another day," Elizabeth continued after seeing that the gentleman was too polite to speak first.

"I must insist that you go home, Mrs Bartell. Your niece is in the right." Mr Walker began to wheel her chair away from the church.

"Then *I* must insist that you accompany us home, since I am so unwell," Mrs Bartell declared, provoking a laugh from both Mr Walker and Elizabeth.

"I wouldn't dream otherwise."

"Mr Walker is a wonderful rector. He gives very short sermons," Mrs Bartell announced as they passed through the church gates and out onto the street.

"You shame me, Mrs Bartell."

"On the contrary, I can think of no better quality in a rector," Elizabeth said, raising a brow at the young man.

"I have an active mind that cannot settle on one idea or the other," he replied.

"A sharp mind and a quick step," Mrs Bartell corrected. "You have left Mrs Smith behind."

Elizabeth and Mr Walker turned in dismay to see Mrs Smith struggling to keep up behind them. They slowed their pace, and Mrs Bartell kept up the conversation for several more minutes until at last they reached St James's Place, only to discover as they approached the red brick town house that a gentleman in a red coat was waiting to greet them at the gate.

"Miss Elizabeth!" said Mr Wickham. "I have just come to call."

"Mr Wickham, what a pleasure, but—"

"I am not fit for callers today," Mrs Bartell exclaimed. "I am unwell."

"Mr Wickham, my great-aunt must be tended to inside, and I am afraid I will have to look forward to our conversation another day." Elizabeth tried to offer her arm to her hostess, but she swatted it away.

"Mr Walker will help me into the house," she insisted, as Mr Wickham gave a polite nod to the rector and a smile and a bow to Elizabeth before walking off.

The old woman refused to take Elizabeth or Mrs Smith's arm, and Mr Walker gallantly walked her up the steps and into the sitting room. There all the other ladies of the house were assembled, Mrs Bennet having returned from her task at the circulating library, and Kitty and Lydia still eating breakfast though it had nearly gone noon.

"Did you like the church, Elizabeth?" Jane asked.

"Was that Mr Wickham in the lane?" Lydia cried, standing at the window as she ate a buttered roll.

"And who is this gentleman?" Mrs Bennet asked, moving out of the comfortable blue velvet chair to make way for Mrs Bartell while beaming with ready approbation at Mr Walker.

Elizabeth made a quick introduction of the rector to her mother. "I am afraid Mrs Bartell swooned in the churchyard this morning, and Mr Walker here was so good as to see her home."

"Such a gentleman!" Mrs Bennet said, approvingly, before sneezing.

"He carried her across the lawn as though she were light as a feather," Mrs Smith said from the corner, eliciting gasps from the youngest ladies in the room. The gentleman stammered as he insisted that he had done no more than any gentleman would and that he should take his leave.

Mrs Bartell safely deposited in her chair and attended to by so many ladies fluttering about, Mr Walker again refused as politely as possible to stay for tea, or for lunch, or for any other event that the two Mrs B's could invent to compel his company. He left with the assurance that he would call tomorrow to see how the lady of the house was faring.

No sooner had the door clicked shut than Kitty declared, "What a handsome man for a rector, I do declare!"

"His figure would be much better suited to a red coat," said Lydia, watching him walk down the lane. "I do not see why younger sons should enter the ministry over the army. Lizzy, why did Wickham not come up?"

"Mr Wickham could hardly come up when Mrs Bartell did not want him to. She has been in ill-health," Elizabeth replied.

"The rector, Walker—does he have a good living?" Mrs Bennet turned to Mrs Bartell, whose eyes were now heavy.

Mrs Bartell shook herself awake, "He is the fourth son of an earl, and he has a good living at that. Did you like him, Lizzy?"

"A lord!" Mrs Bennet exclaimed.

"Lizzy does not like clergymen," Lydia said with a smirk and took another bite of her roll, as Elizabeth insisted that she thought the gentleman everything amiable. Thus satisfied by her answer, Mrs Bartell succumbed to sleep. Mrs Bennet, however, was just beginning her enquiries; even the pains of her cold were not enough to prevent her from pursuing a good match for her impossible second daughter.

"If Mr Walker were to take an interest in you it would be more than you deserve, I am sure, after your dealings with Mr Collins," Mrs Bennet proclaimed. She would have continued thus for some time, but Elizabeth, feeling exhausted by the machinations of the morning, escaped to her room.

ELIZABETH WAS NOT SURPRISED BY MR WICKHAM'S VISIT THE following day, and with him spent a merry hour in the drawing room, playing cards and competing with Lydia for his full attention. It did come as a surprise, however, when Mr Walker also came to call the same afternoon, and then the next. Everyone noticed the attention that both gentlemen paid to Elizabeth, and it became a frequent topic of conversation within the family circle. Mrs Bartell and Mrs Bennet both made clear their disapproval of the officer and preference for the clergyman, while Lydia and Kitty naturally preferred the one with the regimentals. Elizabeth found that her own feelings were not so easy to determine.

She was flattered by Mr Wickham's newfound attachment to *her*. She had thought, because of his near engagement with Miss King, that although he might have wished for a better acquaintance, such a relationship was not in the best interest of either party. But he was amiable, he was charming, and Elizabeth found his company to help restore her happy nature, which had been strained with concern for Jane.

The introduction of the rector was an altogether different sort of problem. He was handsome and amiable, and a student of history who could as easily converse on the subject of the Norman conquest as on the history of the Church of England. She could not deny the allure of a match with a man of position who got on well with her family. He seemed to mind neither her mother's pointed hints nor Mrs Bartell's feigned fainting spells to keep him there for longer, and Elizabeth found herself drawn to his sincere gaze more than she cared to admit.

And so Elizabeth was in a state of confusion when her aunt and uncle Gardiner arrived with their four children. The two older girls were aged six and eight, and the two boys aged two and four. The household was full to bursting now with activity, with everyone wanting to see all the sights.

It was with great pleasure that Jane and Elizabeth took all of the Gardiners out to sea bathe. The children were not so concerned with the benefits for their health as with collecting artefacts from the beach—but everyone seemed to enjoy themselves. The oldest boy peppered Jane and Elizabeth with a great many questions about mermaids and selkies and whether or not an enormous merman with a trident would appear riding on an octopus, to which neither sister had much of a reply other than to encourage his imagination.

Mr Bennet and his brother-in-law found a quiet place by the rocks to sit and enjoy a game of chess. It became a custom between them to walk out together late in the morning and play well into the afternoon. It was on one such afternoon that Elizabeth was able to find a solitary moment to attach herself to Mrs Gardiner, from whom she wished to seek guidance. They walked out together onto the beach, and Elizabeth did her best to relate the events of the last three weeks to her aunt. Mrs Gardiner did not seem surprised at Mr Wickham's attention but did not think that Elizabeth should pay it any mind.

"All things seem possible in Brighton, making young men behave as they should not. However amiable, Mr Wickham will not form a long-lasting attachment to a woman of no fortune. And his engagement to Miss King shows his true intentions, although it was broken up. You know this as well as I, Lizzy."

Elizabeth avoided Mrs Gardner's frank gaze by looking out over the channel, and said that she did.

"Is his regard reserved exclusively for you?"

"He pays me a great many compliments—perhaps next to Lydia. She enjoys monopolising his attention. I cannot help but wonder—and how am I to respond? I do like him."

"My dear, perhaps Mr Wickham's attention to you has been spurred on by your attention from other, much more amiable quarters."

"You are speaking of Mr Walker?"

"Such a handsome young man!" Mrs Gardner said with a little sigh.

"Even you have succumbed! He is very handsome, and he

is… well I don't know what to think! I came here without a real regard for myself—except to…" She paused, not wanting to reveal Mr Darcy's letter or proposal. "Except to find a way to improve things for Jane. I am sorry but the insistence on my marriage to Mr Walker by Mrs Bartell and Mama has been trying on *my* nerves."

Mrs Gardner patted her arm. "Your mother was always quick to jump from acquaintance to marriage. I know it has been trying for you." Mrs Gardiner sighed, "The trip seems not to have done Jane as much good as we hoped."

"Jane does not find as much comfort as I do in nature. She has been tending to Mrs Bartell or running after our youngest sisters, who seem to manage to find a new redcoat at every moment. And also…she was very much in love with Mr Bingley. I cannot think of him without—" and here Elizabeth stopped, once again feeling that to share Mr Darcy's proposal and interference between Mr Bingley and Jane would only serve to complicate matters.

"You know you need not marry Mr Walker," Mrs Gardner said after a pause, "and you certainly should not associate yourself too far with Mr Wickham. I mean that, Lizzy. You cannot encourage him."

Elizabeth bristled. "Is that what I have done?"

Mrs Gardiner gave her a pointed look. "Do you regret not coming with us to Derbyshire instead?"

"Derbyshire!" Elizabeth was caught off guard, "I thought we would have been touring the Lakes."

"That *was* the plan, but because of the unexpected business that needed settling, we could only have ventured out so far. I was looking forward to visiting the scenes of my youth, at Lambton. It has a claim on your interest, however reprehensible, for it is not five miles from Pemberley."

"Five miles from Pemberley!" Elizabeth startled and exclaimed, "But that is the home of Mr Darcy!"

"Would it not have been a fine place to visit?—even though I know you do find its owner rather disagreeable. Perhaps we can visit next year, and you might come with us," Mrs Gardiner said with a smile.

"How close I came to meeting him!" she thought, her heart beating faster at the thought of his unread letter. She was heartily thankful that they had not ventured into that part of the country.

THE SEVEN SISTERS

*W*ith no resolution in her heart as to whether she preferred Mr Wickham to Mr Walker, Elizabeth decided that the surest way to solve her own problems was to deflect all her attention back to cheering Jane. The next morning, she proposed that her aunt and uncle Gardiner plan a day for them to visit the cliffs between Seaford and Eastbourne called the Seven Sisters.

This did not take much convincing, since word of the beauty of the cliffs had lured the Gardiners away from the North in the first place. It was decided that the trip could be taken with very little expense by going from Brighton to Seaford in a post-chaise, limiting the group to four: Mr and Mrs Gardiner, Elizabeth, and Jane. When Kitty declared that such an arrangement showed favouritism, she was reminded by her aunt that Lizzy had intended to go with them on tours for most of the summer, and that Jane deserved a respite from her help in caring for *all* the children of the combined households.

The morning of their outing began cold and windy, but it was declared fair enough to venture out, and nevertheless the party had a good view of the countryside from the post-chaise windows. The yellow carriage was small and meant for three. The sisters did not mind crowding together, although Jane soon declared that Elizabeth would injure her neck from straining to see the valleys of the South Downs as they rode along the coast. She made a good effort to settle herself, the journey to Seaford taking a good two hours in total, only to start up again to see the slope of the valley here, or catch a glimpse of the sea there.

When they arrived in Seaford, a bustling port town, Elizabeth jumped out of the carriage. She was so impatient that she could hardly eat the cold luncheon Mrs Gardiner insisted they buy for fortification before, as last, Mr Gardiner declared that it was time for their walk to view the cliffs.

"Mrs Bartell kept me up late last night going over our route," Mr Gardiner said, "and I still made enquiries to ensure which direction we should go. It is a two mile walk—I know, the distance is nothing to *you*, Lizzy—to the place where we will reach Seaford Head, and if the tide is low, we can walk down to the water and see a spectacular view of the Seven Sisters from there. I have been told to mind the edge along some of our path, and so keep close to avoid taking a tumble."

Elizabeth and Jane knew well enough to heed his advice about the edge but soon took the lead on the path. Elizabeth's eager step far outpaced her aunt's, and Jane was swept along in her sister's enjoyment. At first they could only see stretches of long green grasses, blowing this way and that way in the wind, which had died down, but still threatened to blow away their bonnets if they were not careful. Looking east they could see a blue stretch at the horizon and knew by the sound of the moving waves that they would soon reach the sea.

Nothing could adequately prepare Elizabeth for the sight

of the majestic, rolling series of white chalk cliffs that made up the Seven Sisters. Elizabeth gasped at the sight, quickening her pace when she was able to run out to the pebbly beach, strewn with rocks covered in green seaweed and algae. The peaks of the Seven Sisters lay like a shining crown set against the channel. The sheer cliff-face lay broken off as if at the edge of the earth. Elizabeth waited for Jane to catch up before they counted the seven gentle slopes together. Never had she seen such sharp contrasts of colour—the rich azure water against the white cliffs covered with green grass. And above it all, an endless sky streaked by cirrus clouds.

Here, the beach was free of the throngs of tourists and rows of bathing machines, the swarms of seagulls ready to pounce at the slightest morsel. Elizabeth did not miss the crowds, but she did sigh to think that she could not take advantage of the bathing machine to swim out farther into the channel and gaze at the cliffs from the water. She suggested to Jane instead that they take off their shoes to wade. Thus they spent at least an hour walking up and down the rocky beach, looking for seashells and almost falling in once or twice because of the slippery algae. They managed to stay in the water long enough for their toes to wrinkle, but Elizabeth could not help but stay as long as she could. The beautiful pictures of the sea-people that the children imagined had worked their way into her own thoughts—she liked to think that she was a selkie herself, only in need of her seal skin to let her explore the deep secrets of the ocean.

When the shadows grew longer, Mrs Gardiner called for them from the place where she and Mr Gardiner had been resting on a weathered log. "Will you be ready to go, dears, in half an hour? Though I wish we could stay to see the sunset, we do have a journey back to Brighton, and there is still the walk back to Seaford."

"Nearly ready!" Elizabeth called back and turned conspiratorially to Jane. "Just this last time, we shall walk East towards the Seven Sisters before we turn back."

"We may start our slow return to Seaford now," Mr Gardiner said. "Our legs do not carry us as rapidly as yours."

Elizabeth and Jane waved them off and decided that it would be better to put back on their shoes. They started walking together along the shoreline, until Jane fell a bit behind.

"Oh, Lizzy, you will never want to leave this place, will you?" she teased with a smile. "But I do think we should rejoin our aunt and uncle!"

"You go, I will catch up," Elizabeth insisted, "I promise. As much as I wish I could walk from here all the way to Beachy Head, I will content myself with a final glimpse."

She closed her eyes and breathed in deeply, the salt of the sea in her nostrils and the wind caressing her face. She waved solemnly to the Seven Sisters and then turned back with reluctance, her sister some distance away. Presently, she paused at the sight of a glinting white conical shell amongst the seaweed just ahead. She bent down to retrieve it, marveling at its smooth lines and delicate curve, when she felt her foot lose its grip on the rocks slick with algae and she let out a short exclamation of dismay as she fell backwards onto the beach.

Imagine her surprise to hear a similar cry of alarm just behind her and the sound of rushing footsteps coming towards her.

"Are you quite all right?" came the trembling voice of a young girl.

Elizabeth looked up sheepishly from her place amid the wet seaweed. "I think I am all right, the only thing permanently injured is my pride."

The girl, who was tall and must have been about sixteen, offered her a hand, which Elizabeth eagerly took. The girl pulled, and Elizabeth struggled to find a footing until she was sure—for a moment—that she was back on her feet, when they both slipped at the same time and found themselves sitting opposite each other.

"Well, I am no help at all!" the girl cried.

Elizabeth burst into laughter. "What a disaster! I think we had better try to stand independently of one another—however ungraceful our appearance may be." She saw that Jane had heard their distress and was now approaching. "Wait, wait!" Elizabeth called out to her, "We cannot have you falling into the seaweed, too!" She turned her attention back to her newfound companion, "Oh dear, now I have ruined your fine dress! Are you hurt at all?"

They both scrambled to their feet at the same moment, and Elizabeth tried to assist the girl by brushing her dress.

Jane arrived out of breath. "Are you well, Lizzy?"

"Yes, Jane, but I have injured this beautiful creature." Elizabeth took both of their hands to lead them away from the treacherous patch of rocks.

"I am well," the girl said, smiling shyly to reassure them.

"Are you quite sure?" Elizabeth tried again to brush off her dress.

"Where is your companion?" Jane enquired, "You are not here alone!"

"No, no," the girl replied, seeming to draw herself in. "Here is my brother now."

Elizabeth and Jane turned in the direction the girl indicated and discerned the familiar figure of a tall gentleman walking towards them, concern marking his features. Elizabeth's mouth dropped open in shock.

"Georgiana, are you well?" the gentleman said, not looking at first towards anyone other than his sister "I am sorry to have let you stray so far. I saw you fall and—" He stopped short as his eyes turned and connected with Elizabeth's. "Miss Elizabeth!"

"Mr Darcy!"

Both stood silent, their awkward poses mirroring each other as they shifted their feet. The girl—Georgiana—looked from one to the other in confusion, while Jane was distracted by the sight of another form approaching. Elizabeth was keenly conscious of the state of her wet hair and untidy gown. She had never expected to see Mr Darcy again, let alone in a state like this!

The sound of Mr Bingley's voice broke the silence. "Miss Bennet, Miss Elizabeth! I cannot tell you how delighted— amazed—indeed, words cannot express! This is the last place I should have ever expected to meet you."

For a moment, nothing could be heard but the sound of the crashing waves. Then Jane burst into tears. Anything but concern for Jane flew from Elizabeth's mind, and she and Mr Bingley nearly collided as they rushed to Jane's side. Jane leaned into her sister's arms, and put her head against her shoulder, attempting to wipe the tears away with her hands as quickly as they fell.

"I am so sorry, it seems my sister is unwell—" Elizabeth paused, at a loss for words.

Mr Bingley was distressed. He at first insisted upon taking Jane's arm to help her walk, but when that was denied he continued to walk alongside them, taking off his hat to run his hands through his hair. "Is Miss Bennet well? If only we could offer you the carriage, but we have just finished a day's walk and must meet it in Seaford. I insist that we escort you back to your destination—where are you staying? You cannot mind, Darcy? We must get you all home at once!"

Jane shook her head and attempted a smile, but her face fell again as more tears came, and Elizabeth did her best to speak for her.

"Thank you, Mr Bingley, but we are meant to rejoin our aunt and uncle just ahead and walk back to Seaford, from whence we will return to Brighton."

"But that is where we are going ourselves," Mr Bingley said with some delight, causing a fresh burst of tears from Jane.

"No, no," Elizabeth cried, still supporting Jane, "that will not be necessary."

"There must be something we can do to be of assistance." Mr Darcy's hand was on her elbow, and she turned to see his face with an expression of concern.

"No, I thank you—here are our aunt and uncle now!" Elizabeth pulled away from his hand and walked on.

With Mr Bingley and Mr Darcy and his sister alongside, they made their way up the hill to where Mr and Mrs Gardiner stood waiting. Upon seeing Jane's tears, Mrs Gardiner rushed forward.

"Has something happened, Jane? Lizzy?" she demanded. Jane flew into her arms. Breaking away from the rest of the party, Mrs Gardiner took Jane to walk back towards the village, and Mr Gardiner asked what was the matter.

"I—Jane is—" Elizabeth stammered at first, "I had bent down to retrieve a pretty seashell when I slipped on the rocks and fell! Miss Darcy here," she turned to smile at Georgiana, "was kind enough to try to help me up, but we both fell onto the ground. Jane came to help us up just at the same time as Mr Darcy and Mr Bingley—"

At the sound of the name Bingley, Mr Gardiner's eyebrows shot up and he made a sound that indicated he understood what caused Jane's tears. Elizabeth knew that both he and Mrs Gardiner had felt Jane's despair in London, watching her wait for a call from that gentleman. Mr Gardiner took Elizabeth's arm, patting it before he turned to the two gentlemen and smiled expectantly.

Realising that he was waiting for an introduction, she offered one. "Mr Darcy, Mr Bingley, I thank you for your assistance and can assure you that my sister will be quite well," Elizabeth said, wondering what they would do next, "This is my uncle, Mr Gardiner."

She watched Mr Darcy's face, knowing full well that he would recognise Mr Gardiner as the relation whose position in life was so decidedly beneath his own, and although she saw his eyebrows lift in surprise, she was subsequently astonished when Mr Darcy bowed and said, "It is an honour to make your acquaintance, Mr Gardiner, and I hope we shall meet again under more ordinary circumstances. I assume that you, like ourselves, have come to Seaford to see the cliffs."

Mr Gardiner indicated that they should begin to follow Mrs Gardiner and Jane, who were still walking back towards the village. The early evening was approaching, and the sky was beginning to turn that golden colour that it does a little before sunset. "We did, indeed, come to see the Seven Sisters. In fact, the temptation of the rocks and sea was just compelling enough to pull us away from a planned trip to the North. We might even have strayed into Derbyshire, had not Elizabeth suggested a summer holiday by the sea."

"I have been pulled away from Derbyshire myself at my sister's request to see the sea," Mr Darcy said, "and we have, I hope, fulfilled all of her desires for adventure with our walk today from Eastbourne to Seaford."

Elizabeth, who was simultaneously worried about Jane and wondering at Mr Darcy's easy manner with her uncle, explained with shock "But that is many miles!"

"We have been walking all day!" Mr Bingley said, smiling briefly before once again asking whether they should assist Miss Bennet.

"Our Jane is in the best of hands," Mr Gardiner reassured the young man before turning his attention back to Mr Darcy and Miss Darcy, "I admire your fortitude! I would have made such a journey in my youth, and I am sure Lizzy here could walk still another ten miles, but Mrs Gardiner is not a keen walker and we thought the shorter distance would strike a happy balance."

"Can we offer you refreshment when we arrive in Seaford?" Mr Darcy said as they neared the town, "We must insist that you make use of our carriage. Where are you staying?"

"In Brighton," Elizabeth said, hoping they were not staying there as well, but knowing that they would be. Where else would fashionable gentlemen such as Mr Darcy and Mr Bingley stay?

"We thank you for your generous offer," Mr Gardiner said, seeing Mrs Gardiner waving him over to the post, "but I can see that my wife has everything in hand. I think that after such a long day full of unexpected surprises, it is time for us to part ways."

The party reunited, with Jane offering a faltering smile towards Mr Bingley and Elizabeth before turning back to Mrs Gardiner. Elizabeth said farewell to Mr Darcy and Miss Darcy, apologising once again for ruining Georgiana's dress.

"Miss Elizabeth," Mr Bingley spoke to her one final time, "I must be sure your sister is well. Allow me at least to call tomorrow to enquire after Miss Bennet?"

Heart pounding, Elizabeth turned towards Jane. She saw Jane nod. "Tomorrow, Mr Bingley, we would be delighted to receive you."

ONCE SAFELY BESTOWED IN THEIR POST-CHAISE, JANE BEGAN to recover her composure.

Mrs Gardiner's eyebrows rose. "*That* was the famous Mr

Bingley! Imagine his being here, of all things! What a shock it must be for you, Jane."

"I am ashamed." Jane put her hands up to her cheeks. "I did not know what to think when he happened upon us! Once the tears began, they would not stop! What must he think of me now?"

Elizabeth insisted that she need not be embarrassed. "Mr Bingley felt nothing but concern for your welfare. And he will call tomorrow! You were tired from our day's adventure, it is quite understandable."

Jane said that she was not fatigued. Both Mrs Gardiner and Elizabeth tried to help her relieve those feelings that caused such distress, but to no avail.

"It was a moment of weakness. Every hope, every moment..." she stopped, having regained some control over her emotions, then drew a breath to prevent further tears. "I shall be able to meet him on the morrow with all possible decorum."

Elizabeth felt too much love for her sister to roll her eyes at such an ambitious proclamation, and instead squeezed Jane's shoulder and rested her head against it. This position offered Jane the possibility of feeling that she was giving Elizabeth comfort, and also helped Elizabeth avoid the curious gaze of Mr Gardiner, who was telling Mrs Gardiner about Mr and Miss Darcy.

"Mr Bingley *and* Mr Darcy! Of Pemberley? But Mr Darcy was the gentleman who so abused Mr Wickham! What a curious afternoon." Mrs Gardiner leaned back against the walls of the carriage. "Now *I* am fatigued."

"Mr Darcy was quite polite, I think," Mr Gardiner mentioned with a look towards Elizabeth, "although fashion-able men of his sort can be rather whimsical in their tastes. Perhaps he will not be so eager to meet with us again tomorrow as his friend, now that their walking adventure is at an end."

Elizabeth agreed with her uncle, but did not reply, and the remainder of their trip home was spent in comfortable silence. Elizabeth knew that an onslaught of questions awaited them when her mother discovered that Mr Bingley was in town!

AN IMPROPER PROPOSAL

hey arrived at St James's Street just as the street lamps were being lit, incidentally at the same moment when a large party from the Bennet household and their friends were also returning to Mrs Bartell's. Amongst their group was Mrs Bennet, Mary, Kitty, and Lydia, along with their friends Colonel Forster and his wife, Denny, and Mr Wickham.

"We have just been to the tea gardens!" Lydia proclaimed, leaning on Mr Wickham's arm, "But we have decided to go up for cards and refreshment."

"We all have need of refreshment," Mrs Gardiner said, moving forward to take Lydia away from Mr Wickham. "However, the hour has grown late for entertainment."

"I am afraid that we must postpone any evening activities," Mr Gardiner confirmed. "We have just been to see the Seven Sisters and are quite fatigued after our journey."

"The evening does not have to be spoiled for everyone just because you all went out!" Lydia pouted. Mrs Gardiner whispered something in her ear while leading her up the stairs, but

Lydia tried to shrug her off, saying, "I do not care if Jane was ill!"

"Jane was ill?" Mrs Bennet turned to her oldest daughter, whose face bore some small signs of the tears from earlier in the day. "Whatever has happened?"

"You go in, Mama, I will see them off," Elizabeth said, hoping to avoid a scene of rapture on the street when her mother heard again the name 'Mr Bingley'.

Colonel Forster looked sheepish and apologised for the lateness of the hour, encouraging Mrs Forster to say her good-byes as well. Mr Denny bowed gallantly, but Mr Wickham lingered for a moment on the step to offer Elizabeth a smile.

"The fireworks are not nearly so bright when you are absent," he said.

Elizabeth did not hear the compliment. "My mind cannot comprehend the day we have just had!"

"Where did you travel? Was it another church?" Mr Wickham teased.

"We went to Seaford and saw the view of the white cliffs along the channel. But that is not the reason for my astonishment. You will never guess. I have just seen Mr Darcy!"

Mr Wickham stepped back. "Mr Darcy! What could he be doing here?"

"He is here with his sister," Elizabeth said, her cheeks feeling oddly cold.

Mr Wickham coughed, moving closer again. "Are you certain it was him?"

"Of course, I spoke with him myself! And he is with Mr Bingley."

"And his sister? His sister, here in Brighton? Are you certain—"

"How could I not be certain? Yes, I spoke with them all and it was most assuredly Mr Darcy, his sister, and Mr Bingley."

Mr Wickham fell silent, and Elizabeth was consumed with thoughts of her own. Mr Darcy in Brighton! Why? The situation was intolerable. What was she to say to him? Would he enquire after his letter? What if something important had been conveyed in it—what if he had attempted to renew his addresses, and was expecting her response?

Mr Denny, who was waiting for Mr Wickham in the lane, called to enquire if he was ready to depart, and after saying good night, Elizabeth turned back into the house where she entered the sitting room to find a chorus of exclamations emanating from her mother.

"—what a triumph, after our poor girl had her heart shattered to pieces last year! Now he is returned! Oh Jane, he has come back for you!"

"Not for me, Mama. He is visiting Brighton to see the sea, just as we have come to do," Jane replied, putting a hand to her temple.

"I thought we were all going to bed." Elizabeth declared, making her presence known in the room. "Mama, can you not see that Jane is tired?"

Mrs Bennet was not dissuaded. "And he is to come tomorrow! Oh Jane, this is just as I always said it would be! I knew that he must be in love with you!"

"Mama, you will cause Jane further distress!" Elizabeth protested.

"I am well, Lizzy, I am well. He was very kind and polite, and I think now I know what to expect: the civility and concern of a friend. I can meet him with friendship in return tomorrow," Jane insisted.

"Friendship! But of course you will meet him with more than friendship!" Mrs Bennet moved to squeeze Jane's hands.

"Lizzy is quite right! We have all had enough entertainments for one day, and with the promise of more tomorrow, we should have our dinner and get ourselves to bed!"

After their meal, Mrs Gardiner ushered Jane and Elizabeth up the stairs and into their room. Their aunt fussed over them for some time, ensuring every comfort. Despite their exhaustion, neither sister fell asleep easily, each preoccupied with her astonishment of the day's revelations and uncertain of her feelings about the morrow.

"SHE IS EVEN MORE BEAUTIFUL THAN I REMEMBERED," Bingley said, angling to move a cut shot across the billiards table. "Is there any creature with a sweeter disposition?"

"None," Darcy replied without hesitation, but his own thoughts were preoccupied with the beauty of another woman. Still, it was not her sweetness that drew him.

"Her tears fell like the tears of a very angel from heaven!" declared Bingley, clasping his hands behind his back, waiting for Darcy to take his turn. "Tell me, Darcy, you said that she could not have held me in much regard. But surely her tears meant that she felt something for me, that she felt my absence as I felt hers? Dare I hope?"

Dare I hope? The words echoed in Darcy's thoughts, and he missed the shot. He put a hand on Bingley's shoulder. "Hope, Bingley. I have reason to believe—that is, I am certain that I was wrong in my thinking. I know I was wrong. She came to London last winter. I concealed it from you. I have no doubt now that she came to see you."

Bingley's eyes flashed, and he shrugged off Darcy's hand. "In London last winter—for months? You knew? And Caroline, too, I should wager."

Darcy did not contradict him. "I was wrong, though I believed I was acting in your interest. I told myself it was in your interest. I am sorry."

"You, then, must support me in putting it right," Bingley said. "We will call on them tomorrow."

Darcy's heart caught in his throat, Elizabeth's look of surprise flashing in his memory. What did she think of him, now that she knew the truth? Would she see now that he was changed, that he took her admonition to heart?

"Tomorrow," Darcy agreed, "we shall put it right."

EVERYONE WOKE LATE THE NEXT MORNING, EVEN ELIZABETH.

"You are all much too fashionable!" Mrs Bartell complained as she watched them eat, "Rising when half the day is gone. How will you get anything done?"

"Oh look! It is Mr Wickham coming down the lane again!" Lydia said, standing at her customary position by the window.

"What?" Elizabeth exclaimed, "Mr Wickham! At this hour?"

Only a moment later Mrs Smith came into the sitting room to announce that Mr Wickham was requesting the company of Miss Elizabeth in the garden.

"Why should he want to speak to Lizzy?" Lydia cried.

"Mr Wickham can have nothing to say to Lizzy. She is expecting Mr Walker later," Mrs Bennet proclaimed.

"I am not expecting *anybody* in particular." Elizabeth rose with some curiosity, walking out to the garden where Mr Wickham awaited her. She noticed with irritation that Lydia and Kitty stood at the window looking down forlornly in their direction.

"Good morning, Miss Elizabeth." Mr Wickham's smile was as always ready. "And how are you on this fine day?"

"I am well, Mr Wickham, but surprised to see you again so soon," Elizabeth replied.

"Miss Bennet—" Wickham unexpectedly reached forward to take her hand and led her away from the garden and into the alley, "Miss Elizabeth—Elizabeth, please, I have something to say to you. I have been awake all night thinking only of this, only of you."

"Mr Wickham," Elizabeth replied, hardly knowing what to say, "you are not yourself today. If you would allow me to—"

"Please," he said, silencing her, "I came here with a purpose in mind, knowing the risk it would entail. Knowing how the expression of my feelings towards you has been so unfairly cut off because I was brought so low by *that* person whose name I do not need to repeat. Business is calling me suddenly to the North. I am to depart immediately."

Elizabeth was rendered absolutely silent.

"I have come to feel," Mr Wickham continued, encouraged by her silence, "a strong and irrepressible regard for you. Come away with me, Elizabeth! We could go to Gretna Green." He moved his hands to her arms, stepping closer. His breath was warm on her cheek.

Gretna Green? Elizabeth jolted and pulled away from him. "Mr Wickham! I—"

"Can you deny that you feel something for me? Have I been so completely misguided in my interpretation of your feelings?"

It was too much. Elizabeth's *feelings* had been tried too many times over the course of the last twenty-four hours. "I did not ask for, nor encourage, any such feelings from you. I enjoy your company; we have been friends. I..."

She could not deny there had been an attachment on her side. He reached for her again, but she recoiled. "I cannot leave with you, Mr Wickham. To elope? To elope under *any* circumstance is out of the question. I cannot imagine what you must think of me even to suggest it."

Mr Wickham withdrew his hand, his demeanour cold. "What has he said to you?"

"Who?"

"You force me to say his name aloud? Of course it is Mr

Darcy! He has said something, some grand falsehood, and has tarnished my name! I cannot go anywhere, I cannot do anything, but this man—this *revolting* man—chooses to haunt my footsteps. And what did he say of me to make you so heartless? Of course, you would prefer a man of his stature, his respectability!"

"Mr Darcy has said nothing to me! We have not spoken more than ten words to each other since...since we met in April." Elizabeth felt a hot flash of anger burn through her, disliking Wickham's presumption and present audacity.

"Mr Walker, then, has won your affections. A man in the position that I was meant to assume. A man most likely to replace me in your esteem. Of course you would put me aside for him."

"Sir, you presume too much."

"Yes, indeed, I thought you were better than the rest. But I was mistaken. You, Miss Bennet, are no better than *he* is," Mr Wickham cried, and with a jerky bow, left her alone in the lane.

Elizabeth walked back to the garden and sank onto the steps. She did not understand what had just taken place. What had Mr Wickham to be afraid of where Mr Darcy was concerned? For afraid he surely had been, and that fear had made him imprudent.

At length, she calmed her emotions enough to return to the house and climb the stairs to the room where the family still sat eating their breakfast, and Kitty and Lydia both rushed over to demand what Mr Wickham had said to her.

Elizabeth brushed them aside to sit next to Mrs Bartell and disregarded their questions. Her heart was still hammering in her chest, but she felt that she looked calm enough not to arouse suspicion from Jane or Mrs Gardiner. Fortunately, Mrs Bennet was happy enough to command the attention of the room to express her joy over Mr Bingley's arrival, which she was sure would be imminent.

"You did right to wear your blue sash, Jane. For Mr Bingley to be here in Brighton? I think it could not be a coincidence. Such things never happen without a purpose. Why, he must have returned to Netherfield and discovered where we were! I cannot believe our good fortune! Imagine, five thousand pounds a year!"

Mrs Gardiner and Jane were silent, and so Elizabeth felt compelled to temper her mother's spirits. "Mama! If Mr Bingley came to town with the express purpose of seeing Jane, then why has he not called on us before this?"

"I am sure that he has only just arrived! It was by chance that they met yesterday afternoon."

"We do not know what his intentions might be. Cannot a man travel with a party of friends?"

Mrs Bennet was fascinated by this piece of information. "Travelling with friends, was he? You breathed not a word of it! What a fine thing for our other girls! With whom?"

"It was Mr Darcy and his sister," Elizabeth replied with some hope that this would work to dampen Mrs Bennet's effusions.

"I had almost forgotten," Jane turned her head to the side, looking with curiosity at Elizabeth. "She was quite kind to you, Lizzy, trying to help you after your fall."

"Mr Darcy, indeed," Mrs Bennet sniffed, her hopes of the rest of her girls being settled with Bingley's undoubtedly wealthy friends dimming. "Well, *that* is nothing to be happy about. I do hope Mr Bingley does not bring him along when he comes to visit—what a disagreeable man."

Mrs Bennet continued thus for some time, abusing Mr Darcy, to which no one objected, and praising Mr Bingley, which caused discomfort for all. At length, after receiving no further encouragement, she grew tired of her own pronouncements and, with a kiss to her Jane's forehead, left them to speak to Mr Bennet. Her departure drew a sigh of relief from Jane, and a cry of anguish from her sister.

"I am sorry, Jane, for how she causes you such pain." Elizabeth rose from her seat to pace the room.

"She means well. She does not know how it distresses me," Jane replied, her countenance serene in contrast to her tears yesterday.

It was with some frustration that Elizabeth realised she would have to wait to tell Jane of Mr Wickham's rather scandalous proposal. Not having come to terms with her feelings on the matter herself, she did not want to disturb Jane as the entire household anxiously awaited Mr Bingley's visit. Glancing at her aunt Gardiner, she knew that she would not be able to seek out her advice on the subject either—for how could she relate the tale without some reference to Mr Darcy's letter? That would require revealing more than she wanted.

THE SEASHELL RETURNED

*M*rs Bennet was not disappointed; Mr Bingley arrived at their door to call that afternoon. Mrs Bartell was upstairs napping in her room, but the rest of the family were about to sit down to tea. With him came Mr Darcy, as grave and imposing as ever, and Miss Darcy. They were shown into the sitting room with ceremony and circumstance, Mrs Smith having been informed of the very important guests expected to arrive.

Mrs Bennet smiled most graciously, "We are so happy, indeed, that you should happen to be in Brighton at the same time as ourselves. Nothing could be more delightful! There were those who had quite given up hope of ever seeing you again, but of course that was absurd, for I was sure you never intended to give up Netherfield entirely."

Mr Bingley removed his eyes from Jane's flushed face for long enough to say that his plans were not yet fixed, but he hoped to return in the autumn for the shooting season.

"May I enquire after your health, Miss Bennet?" said Mr Darcy, who had not as yet been asked to take a seat.

"I am feeling much better, thank you, Mr Darcy," replied Jane, with a quick glance at Elizabeth before returning her eyes to Mr Bingley's. Mrs Bennet was then obliged to greet Mr Darcy politely as well, however reluctant she was to do it.

Introductions were made with such a flurry of movement at once that it was impossible to keep everyone together. The sitting room, already too small for the large party, felt even more cramped with the addition of the three guests. While Mrs Bennet busied herself with making Mr Bingley comfortable, Mr Darcy approached Elizabeth where she stood by Mrs Gardiner. She did her best not to meet his gaze.

"Miss Elizabeth." He bowed somewhat stiffly but smiled in a way she was not used to seeing.

"Mr Darcy," she replied, attempting to turn her mouth upwards. She hoped it was more of a smile than a grimace. She looked for signs on his countenance as to whether he desired anything in particular from her—was he expecting an answer to any questions he may have put forth in his letter?

"You have already met my sister, Georgiana, I believe?" he continued, with a distinct eagerness in his voice.

Here, Elizabeth could not help but smile. "Yes," she said, and moved her gaze to the quiet girl beside him. "You bravely tried to rescue me from my unfortunate position and I pulled you to the ground! I hope you do not suffer from any ill effects, Miss Darcy?"

"No, indeed, Miss Elizabeth," came the timid reply. Mrs Gardiner, who appeared to comprehend the girl's uneasiness, invited her to sit down on the sofa next to her. Mr Darcy seemed gratified by her aunt's kind gesture, and Elizabeth wondered at his comfort with a woman who lived in Cheapside.

"I am glad to see that you are sufficiently recovered, Miss Darcy, after your misadventure with my niece," Mrs Gardiner said with a gentle laugh, and from there proceeded to enquire after Derbyshire, a location dear to both their hearts.

For the next half hour, Elizabeth was subjected to an animated discussion of that part of the country and its particular beauties. She noted with surprise that Mr Darcy was speaking more warmly and more openly than she had ever seen him do before. She wondered what could have been the cause for this easiness, for, indeed, *she* felt more uncomfortable than she had felt before in her life. For every one of his smiles, she thought of his letter—a full two pages and the envelope covered in writing—and regretted what she had done. Oh, that she might only have looked at it!

Her thoughts strayed to Mr Wickham's accusation that Mr Darcy had said something to influence her. With a jolt, it occurred to her that Mr Darcy might have written something to explain his dealings with Mr Wickham. But what could it have been? She had been so certain of Mr Wickham's good character—she thought she could trust his word. But his conduct this morning was not that of a man who could be trusted.

Mr Darcy's thoughts she could only imagine. She hoped that she did not seem out of spirits, for that would never do. She could not bring herself to speak often and allowed her aunt and uncle Gardiner to carry on the conversation.

The steady flow of voices was interrupted when Mrs Bartell entered the room. "I do declare!" she said. "Who are all these people?"

Mrs Bennet was affronted by this rude interruption and at first tried to hustle her out of the room. But Mrs Bartell would have none of that. "Mrs Bennet! Far be it from me to expect an introduction to strangers in my own house, but I *was* hoping that one of the Miss Bennets would take me out for a walk!" She spoke loudly over Mrs Bennet's fussing.

"Oh, Kitty, do take her out, make haste! You have nothing else to do." Mrs Bennet waved her hands in exasperation.

"Kitty will not do," objected Mrs Bartell.

Mrs Bennet would never ask such a thing of Lydia, who seemed to have disappeared for the moment in any case, and Mary was not a great walker. The task fell to Elizabeth, who was very glad to have an excuse for escape.

That feeling was ruined, however, when Mr Darcy rose and approached Mrs Bartell. "If you are so inclined, madam, I should be happy to accompany you, along with Miss Elizabeth."

Mrs Bartell appeared disgruntled. "I suppose you may if you feel you must. Are you as good a walker as Elizabeth?"

Mr Darcy's mouth twitched, "I would never claim to be, madam, though I shall do my best."

Mrs Bartell croaked a laugh, "That is the sort of response I should have expected from a young man like you!"

Elizabeth was mortified, certain that nothing could possibly make the situation worse. Her mother was making a grand display of all her silliness in front of Mr Bingley, Lydia was no doubt off gallivanting with the officers, and their hostess, Mrs Bartell, felt no qualms at talking down to her betters.

The most peculiar thing of all was that Mr Darcy did not seem to mind. He helped the old woman into her chair, and, taking her hand, introduced himself. Mrs Bartell was not satisfied with only his last name and enquired what was his first —*Fitzwilliam*—and where was he from—*Pemberley, in Derbyshire*. Those particulars at last settled, Mr Darcy dismissed Mrs Smith from her duties of pushing the chair, saying he could do that himself.

Elizabeth remembered with concern his timid sister, Georgiana, and looked over to where she was sitting with Mrs Gardiner. Miss Darcy smiled at her shyly, and then nodded to her brother, who was also looking in that direction. She seemed perfectly content to remain where she was, and Mr Darcy was satisfied. They set out for the beach at a brisk pace, and in relative silence.

It was Mr Darcy who spoke first. "How do you like Brighton, Miss Elizabeth?"

"Very well, thank you. I believe it has been called London-by-the-Sea for its great society and amusements."

"My sister, Georgiana, had never been to this part of the country. She has always loved the sea."

"The sea," Mrs Bartell put in, "is very beneficial to one's health!"

"It is beautiful. This is the first time I have visited," Elizabeth managed to say. They left the streets and now approached the channel. The sound of the waves and scent of the sea worked as a balm for Elizabeth's soul. She found herself saying, "I did not believe any stories about the call of the sea before coming here, but now I can see why one might return, year after year, to see its breadth and hear the crashing waves."

"The sea is always singing," Mrs Bartell nodded.

Mr Darcy paused to reach into a pocket of his coat and withdrew a white shell. He turned to Elizabeth, his face not displaying any particular emotion and said, "I believe this is yours."

She took the conical shell, recognising its delicate curves. "Thank you."

"Oh, what a lovely gesture—how kind of Mr Darcy to have kept it for you! So thoughtful. And he is an excellent walker—nearly so as *Mr* Walker, whom I see just ahead! You will have your choice now, Elizabeth, between two most handsome men. Mrs B will die of happiness."

"Mrs Bartell!" Elizabeth gasped, feeling ill with mortification. "Mr Darcy did not mean anything by returning my shell to me, I assure you."

Mr Darcy gave her a look that she could only suppose was

pained, and her heart sank as she saw that, indeed, Mr Walker was rapidly approaching them.

"Happily met," declared the gentleman, all smiles. "I was just coming to see you! But I see you have no need of my services today."

Mrs Bartell offered him her hand. "Mr Walker, this is Mr Darcy of Pemberley in Derbyshire, one of Miss Elizabeth's prior acquaintances. He is just as keen a walker as you!"

Mr Walker looked from Elizabeth's face, which burned with humiliation, to Mr Darcy's stony one, and his smile faltered even as he touched the brim of his hat and nodded to Mr Darcy, expressing his delight in the ill-given introduction.

"Shall we go together back to the house, then? Or should I call another day?" He asked genially.

"Do not leave on my account," Mr Darcy suddenly declared, looking at Elizabeth, "for we were soon departing."

"We?" Mr Walker seemed curious.

"The house is full of strangers," Mrs Bartell said, "children and aunts and uncles, and a Mr Bingley who appears taken with Jane." Mr Walker also looked at Elizabeth, who was avoiding Mr Darcy's gaze, and then appeared to notice the gentleman's eyes on him. He met Darcy's glare with a carefully blank look for what seemed like ages but could only have been seconds.

"Tomorrow! I will call again tomorrow and am so happy to see you in such health, Mrs Bartell. Miss Elizabeth, Mr Darcy—welcome to Brighton. I bid you all good day."

Mr Walker thus dispatched, the three turned back, and the rest of the time was spent in silence. Upon their return to the house, Mr Darcy informed everyone that his party must go. Mr Bingley departed most reluctantly, whilst Miss Darcy seemed glad to be returned to her brother's presence. Every promise was made that they would return on the morrow to go out walking on the beach.

With the loss of their company, the mood of the house flattened. Mrs Bennet had outdone herself. She was exhausted and, after only a few moments of relating to Jane her many predictions about the happy outcome of her dearest dreams, retired to her chamber. Kitty seemed to have disappeared to wherever Lydia had got herself. Mr Bennet had escaped into the library at the first hint of company, and Mr Gardiner now joined him. Jane, Elizabeth, and their aunt were left to themselves, with Mary in the corner reading and Mrs Bartell dozing in her chair.

"Well, Lizzy, I am afraid that you have an explanation to give!" began Mrs Gardiner, "Is this the proud Mr Darcy of whom you spoke so disdainfully? To be sure, he is not so handsome as Wickham; or, rather, he has not Wickham's countenance, for his features are perfectly good. But how came you to tell me that he was so disagreeable?"

"Aunt, he is—" Elizabeth considered her words, marvelling at the changed Mr Darcy. "I have never seen him in such ease! Believe me when I say that he is usually very disagreeable."

"Even I have never seen him so eager to please." Jane directed a sly look at Elizabeth that was not unnoticed by Mrs Gardiner.

"Now, Jane, Lizzy. There is more to this than meets the eye."

"There is nothing to speak of. I cannot account for his politeness given his previous disdain for those he considered beneath him." Elizabeth sighed. "Everywhere he goes, he causes grief."

"Lizzy!" cried Jane.

"These are harsh words. But you are speaking of his behaviour towards Wickham. Is it possible that there was some mistake, a misunderstanding?" Mrs Gardiner pressed. "This first impression is very favourable. He was imposing at first, but his sister was such a delightful young girl, and after all—"

"After all?" Elizabeth raised her eyebrows.

"I do think that there was a misunderstanding, there has to have been," Jane looked as if she wanted to say more, but Elizabeth shook her head in warning.

"Well," Mrs Gardiner spoke matter-of-factly, "with Mr Bingley sure to call every day from now until who knows when"—now it was Jane's turn to blush—"you may have to resign yourself to spending some time in Mr Darcy's company. For he seems to prefer yours to anyone else's, Lizzy."

Mary now spoke from her corner, "I have always thought Mr Darcy to be a most proper and dignified gentleman. What does it matter whether he wished to dance? I do not care for dancing at all."

"Thank you, Mary." Elizabeth regretted her short tone immediately and turned the conversation to Mr Bingley. They could not gather any new information from Jane, but noted that her demeanour seemed livelier, and a soft smile played at the corners of her lips throughout the evening. Elizabeth was not ready to hope that the outcome this time would prove better than the first. She feared that now Mr Bingley had come to call, and Mr Darcy had realised that his friend intended to renew his addresses to Jane, they would remove from Brighton. To own the truth, she almost wished it, were it not for the fact that her sister's happiness was more important than her desire to avoid meeting Mr Darcy again.

DARCY THOUGHT OF THE TINGE OF PINK CREEPING UP HER neck and cheek, her averted gaze. Was she already so attached to the other gentleman, the one with the happy manners so suited to a lively, happy temperament such as hers? He could put his best foot forward, to show her his own altered behaviour, but was it too late? Her greeting to him this morning had been cold and her demeanour aloof. Was his company but an interference in her pursuit of happiness with another?

He straightened the collar of his coat and was promptly jolted out of his musings by the voice of Bingley's sister.

"The Bennets are *here*?" cried Caroline, as they readied to walk to the gardens for the evening's fireworks. "But I suppose we will not be much in the same circles."

"I had it from Mrs Bennet that they will attend the assembly at the Castle Inn this Saturday," said Bingley.

Caroline dropped her fan. "Charles, surely you did not *call!* The Castle Inn—but we cannot show our faces there, for we are engaged to attend the assemblies at the Old Ship. You cannot imagine us showing our faces anywhere but *there*."

"I am afraid I am already engaged to do so. You, dear sister, can do as you like. We called at the Bennets' only this morning and spent an hour reacquainting ourselves with the many Miss Bennets and even some new friends—a Mr and Mrs Gardiner from Gracechurch Street. Mr Gardiner was a fine fellow."

"I liked Mrs Gardiner," said Georgiana, bending down to retrieve Caroline's fan. "And Miss Elizabeth. She was so kind. Such pretty eyes!"

Darcy swallowed, momentarily losing himself in the memory of those depths. Georgiana was already drawn to her. Could he bear to be in Elizabeth's company if she truly was attached to another? It was impossible.

Caroline took the fan and closed it with a snap and a look towards Mr Darcy. "I must confess that I never could see any beauty in her. And as for her eyes, which have sometimes been called so fine, I could never see anything extraordinary in them."

Darcy stayed silent, and so Caroline continued, "I remember, when we first knew her in Hertfordshire, how amazed we all were to find that she was a reputed beauty, and I particularly recollect your saying one night, after they had been dining at Netherfield, '*She* a beauty!—I should as soon call her mother a wit.' But afterward she seemed to improve on you, and I believe you thought her rather pretty at one time."

"Yes," replied Darcy, who could contain himself no longer, "but *that* was only when I first saw her, for it is many months since I have considered her as one of the handsomest women of my acquaintance."

With a pang, he thought of all between them that remained unsaid. He could not give way for another—not until he knew for sure which way her heart turned, or whether it might ever turn towards him. He went out of the house, and Miss Bingley was left to all the satisfaction of having forced him to say what gave no one any pain but herself.

THE NEXT MORNING, LYDIA ANNOUNCED SULLENLY AT breakfast that Mr Wickham had left for Town. A great deal of speculation was thrown about at the table—Mr Bennet's being that he left to elope with a mysterious heiress—which caused Elizabeth to drop her fork in surprise at her father's half-accuracy. The conclusion come to by Mrs Bennet was that Wickham was a horrid man who trifled with her girls' hearts, and she was not sorry to see him go. At this, Lydia and Kitty both burst into tears and left the table. Jane could hardly contain her concern. She suggested a walk out with Elizabeth.

"Lizzy!" she said, once alone, "You do not seem surprised by this news of Mr Wickham."

Elizabeth shook her head, "No, indeed, I am not, for he informed me of it himself."

"And you are not upset? I had thought—"

"Yes, and so had I. Jane, he proposed to me!"

Jane let out a strangled laugh of astonishment. "This I cannot believe. He never seemed serious in any of his attentions. And I know that you liked him, but I did not think you to be serious, either!"

"No, no. I do not think he was, but it was worse—he proposed an elopement! I could not do anything other than refuse. I found that I had no desire to marry him, and certainly never under such circumstances as an elopement."

"But why leave so suddenly?"

"I do not know. I told him of our meeting with Mr Darcy, and he seemed surprised. Then, the next moment he declared that he had to leave on business, and he proposed I accompany him to Gretna Green. It was so strange. He did not even say that he loved me."

"He must have loved you to wish to marry you. Oh, poor Mr Wickham!"

"There is another point I do not understand. He suggested that my refusal was caused by Mr Darcy. That Mr *Darcy* said something to me which would cause me to refuse him! I understand that Mr Darcy has behaved abominably to him, unforgivably, but why should he jump about at any mention of the very name of Darcy?" Elizabeth was silent for a moment. "I cannot think why he proposed to me at all."

Jane could offer no satisfactory explanation, and the two were forced to spend the remainder of their walk trying to speak of something else.

MR WALKER WAS NOT LONG PUT OFF AFTER HIS ENCOUNTER with Elizabeth and Mr Darcy the morning before and made good on his promise to stop by the following day. Elizabeth was happy to see him and said so. She could not help but think, as she looked at his smiling face, how kind his manners were, how open.

"How easy you are to talk to, Mr Walker," she said with a smile of her own. "Indeed, you should have come back to the house yesterday."

"I am glad to think I am so welcome, but have no desire to compete for attention," Mr Walker's face betrayed not a hint of embarrassment.

"Mr Darcy's manners are very proud," Elizabeth insisted, "do not let him put you off again."

"I will not if you so command," Mr Walker declared, and Elizabeth laughed with delight even as Mrs Bartell protested.

"Indeed, Mr Darcy was most gentleman-like! He paid Elizabeth a great compliment walking out with her. I think you *both* very agreeable."

"Your good opinion, madam, is all that I need." Mr Walker sent a look towards Elizabeth that seemed to suggest he sought approval from another direction.

After Mr Walker took tea and regaled the household for a merry hour, paying particular attention to Elizabeth, he went on his way, and Mrs Bennet wondered when Mr Bingley would come.

"What care we for Mr Bingley," Lydia snorted, "when Lizzy is in love?"

Elizabeth threw her hands up in exasperation. "You would do well to keep your thoughts on love to yourself, Lydia."

"What does love have to do with it if a lovely young man like Mr Walker should ask for her hand?" cried Mrs Bennet, "It would be more than she deserves, the ungrateful girl!"

"Mr Walker plays chess well enough," Mr Bennet put forth. "He lasted all of five minutes."

Elizabeth rolled her eyes. "Does anyone else have an opinion?"

"Well, I like him," Mrs Gardiner looked slyly at Elizabeth,

"but I also like the other gentleman who came yesterday—Mr Darcy. *He* is not at all what I expected."

"Oh, such a proud, disagreeable man!" Mrs Bennet exclaimed. "If he were not Mr Bingley's particular friend, I should not even invite him into the house!"

"The household universally reviles Mr Darcy, Mrs Gardiner," said Mr Bennet. "You would do well never to mention his name."

Mrs Bartell woke from her nap to speak from her spot in the blue velvet chair. "Whose name?"

"Mr Darcy's," answered Mr Gardiner.

"What? Speak up!"

"*Mr Darcy's*," shouted Lydia, snorting again. "We all hate Mr Darcy because Lizzy says so, and we love Mr Walker for her sake, too. Lizzy, have you not always wanted to be a clergyman's wife?"

"Nonsense. Miss Elizabeth has her choice between two handsome men," Mrs Bartell declared.

Elizabeth stood. "I am going for a walk."

"You might miss Mr Bingley!" Mrs Bennet protested, but Elizabeth had already gone to lose herself for a few moments in the crashing of the waves and the limitless horizon.

MR BINGLEY DID NOT FAIL MRS BENNET: HE CAME TO CALL shortly after Mr Walker's departure and remained for an entire two hours. He returned the following day and the next, with a promise to see them at the ball on Saturday. This brought an endless well of comfort to Mrs Bennet, who was now certain that soon all of her hopes and dreams for Jane would be realised. Elizabeth, for her part, was relieved to see the return of her sister's happy spirits. In private she remained guarded, careful not to allow herself to be injured should Mr Bingley withdraw his attentions.

But in company, Jane smiled more, with warmth demonstrated towards Mr Bingley that could not be misconstrued. With each one of her smiles, her suitor's confidence grew. Elizabeth felt that Mr Bingley could in no way be in doubt of her sister's affections. She was both glad for her sister and afraid for her.

Mr Darcy was another matter altogether. He came each time with his friend, once with his sister, and once alone. It was from Miss Darcy that Elizabeth learned Miss Bingley and Mr and Mrs Hurst were also in town but were too busy to call —a fact that did not surprise Elizabeth but seemed to surprise Mr Darcy's sister.

Mr Darcy himself mystified Elizabeth. His attendance at Mrs Bartell's house gave the impression that he was as constant as Mr Bingley, a fact that made her aunt and uncle Gardiner suppose more than they ought about the nature of his intentions towards *herself*. But what Elizabeth felt certain of —that no one else could or did know—was that Darcy's purpose was to ascertain his friend's attachment and make a new judgment, one that was sure to influence Jane's happiness forever.

Recalling the afternoon of his proposal and the harsh words exchanged, she could not help but wonder if he had taken her rebuke to heart. What else could his continued presence indicate but that he might have seen himself to be in the wrong?

His manners towards her family were nothing like she imagined they would be—he conversed easily with Mr Gardiner and even encouraged the entire party to plan a trip to the nearby South Downs to see more of the countryside as well as the famed Devil's Dyke. With *her,* however, he was often silent. She supposed that this was preferable to long conversations, or worse, a renewal of his addresses—but she felt certain that his silence in her presence indicated he had no

intention of renewing those addresses, and that his presence
was entirely for the sake of Mr Bingley.

Given her own mother's tendency towards absolute rude-
ness directed at Mr Darcy, Elizabeth resolved to bear his
company for Jane's sake, and more than that, to distract him
from Mrs Bennet's gaze as often as was necessary. She could
bear his silence, she thought, with equanimity.

This resolve held fast until the evening of the assembly at
Castle Inn. The Castle Inn was a grand old red brick building
with an even grander ballroom. Lydia noted with disapproval
that there were not enough officers in attendance, and in
general she was not incorrect to point out that the number
gathered there seemed rather old and grey. Mrs Bartell indig-
nantly insisted that the Castle Inn was the only place to
frequent assemblies for good company, serving further to
prove Lydia's point. Still, the room found itself gratified by
the presence of the most fashionable company it had seen in a
few years upon the arrival of Mr Bingley and his party—the
very same party with whom he arrived at the assembly room at
Meryton last year.

Elizabeth noted with approval that Miss Darcy was not in
attendance, her absence contrasting with the boisterous
frivolity of her two youngest sisters. They could not seem to
help but draw unwanted attention from all corners even in a
sparse room. At least, she thought, it was not a crush as she
imagined it must be at the Old Ship. Mr Bingley's attention to
Jane was a light that burned for all to see. His sisters even
deigned to greet Jane, albeit coolly, though they offered no
such greeting to Elizabeth or her mother. Elizabeth thought Mr
Darcy might stay within his usual circle this time, until he
approached her and asked for her hand for not one, but *two*
sets.

After spending the entire first dance in silence, she had to
know what Mr Darcy was about.

"Why are you so silent, Mr Darcy? Do you disapprove of Brighton?" she began, at the start of the set, trying to laugh.

"No, indeed," came the reply.

"It must be the music, then, for I know how you despise dancing."

"It is a lively tune well-suited to the occasion."

Elizabeth averted her gaze as they came together and touched hands. She knew, then, that it was her company that caused Darcy grief. He had loved her, once. Or at least, he thought he loved her. Why, then, would he persist in being closer to her, unless…?

"Well, Mr Darcy, I cannot then account for your silence," she lied. "You must have something to say!"

"Must you always have me talking? I am not so good at it as you seem to think." He returned her smile disarmingly, if only for a moment.

"You have not been practising?"

"Have you?" he raised a brow. "We have not heard you play since meeting again."

"Oh, no, let us not turn the conversation towards the pianoforte!" Elizabeth laughed.

Their hands met again as the musicians rang out their last notes, and this time Elizabeth dared to meet his gaze. She did not falter, though what she saw made her shiver a bit inside.

They walked off to meet Mrs Bartell, who demanded to know the subject of their conversation.

"Practice, Mrs Bartell," cried Elizabeth, her spirits rising. "Mr Darcy does not consider himself able to converse easily in the company of strangers. And I do not perform well on the pianoforte. We are testing each other to see which of us has improved ourselves more over the last few months."

"Mr Darcy not able to converse easily? Ridiculous! Mr Darcy," she turned in her chair to look up at him, "just because you do not chatter like some parrot does not mean that you are deficient in any way."

Mr Darcy bowed, and Elizabeth thought he looked pleased.

"Surely you would not consider yourself to be among strangers here, in any case," Elizabeth said, and he turned to her with the hint of a smile.

"I would not consider you as such," he replied. It was a moment before he spoke again, "And what of you? My sister should like to hear you play."

"Your sister? Is she not the one who plays magnificently?"

"She is an excellent performer when she overcomes her fears. Perhaps you might encourage her?"

"Ah, I understand. You are hoping that once she hears my abominable playing, she will realise her own superiority?" Elizabeth could barely keep the corners of her mouth straight, particularly as she saw alarm spread over his features

"No, no, indeed!" Mr Darcy stammered, "I do not mean for you to misunderstand me—"

"Do not distress yourself, Mr Darcy," Mrs Bartell put in, "Elizabeth is always teasing those she is fond of."

"You must play this evening, Miss Elizabeth," he said, relaxing a little.

Elizabeth felt her cheeks warm as Mr Darcy looked over at her. "You jest, Mr Darcy!"

"Splendid!" Mrs Bartell exclaimed.

"But your sister is not here, Mr Darcy, and shall not benefit from my performance." Elizabeth thought she had found a clever way out.

"I am sure Miss Darcy shall hear you play at one time or another before the summer is out. We are so often in company," said Mrs Bartell.

"With everything settled between you, you might as well choose the song," Elizabeth grumbled.

"'Starry Eyed Lassie'," said Mr Darcy and Mrs Bartell at once, and the matter was settled.

"MR DARCY," ELIZABETH SAID TO JANE THAT EVENING, "IS insufferable!"

"Has he insulted you again?"

"No, not by any means," Elizabeth sighed. "I cannot make out his behaviour at all. While you are walking about bliss-fully with your Mr Bingley—"

Jane protested that he was not *her* Mr Bingley.

"—I entertain Mr Darcy. No one will relieve me of my suffering—only occasionally our aunt, for Uncle Gardiner will not forgo his chess game to grant me any relief."

"What does he do to distress you so?"

"He is very…serious."

"And so am I, Lizzy! Not everyone is as inclined to laugh as you," Jane said.

"But you are always smiling. Mr Darcy rarely smiles. And tonight I was put upon to play at his insistence!"

"Perhaps he likes you."

"No, I am sure he cannot—after all that has passed between us—and I do not like him! He knows I do not!"

"You do not?" Jane smiled slyly, and Elizabeth threw a pillow at her.

"No! Consider his treatment of Wickham—"

"Wickham? Lizzy, I am now certain that there is some mistake. For when I mentioned him to Mr Bingley—"

"Jane!"

"—I only mentioned that he recently left the county. Mr Bingley was glad of it and asked me not to mention his name in front of Mr Darcy or his sister in particular."

"Mr Darcy's sister? Whyever not?"

"I do not know why. I do not think even Mr Bingley

knows any details, but consider his behaviour towards you. There must be some kind of mistake, some grave misunderstanding between them, for I cannot believe that Mr Darcy is so very bad."

Elizabeth paused and considered. "I do not think there could be any misunderstanding. It must be either that Mr Wickham is telling the truth, or that he is telling a falsehood. It cannot be both. It must be one or the other."

Jane took her sister's hand, "What if Mr Darcy is still in love with you?"

"Do not say that! How shall I ever face him tomorrow?"

"Why do you not ask him the details of his association with Mr Wickham?"

"Never!" Elizabeth rose from the bed, "I could not do that without revealing to him that I have not read his letter!"

"Perhaps he will understand?"

"He is not the sort of man who is used to people failing to accede to his requests. I do not think he could ever forgive me."

"If you do not like him, then why should it matter whether he forgives you or not?"

"I—" Her mouth hung open for a moment, realising how neatly her sister had trapped her, before she shut it and began again, "I do not know."

"Then ask him! Mr Wickham has been well-pleased to speak of the Darcys with you. Mr Darcy might be just as pleased for the opportunity to defend himself."

"No," Elizabeth considered the idea. "No, I will not ask him. I will endeavour to be civil—I will play for him, I will smile and laugh! But it is all for your sake. If only Mr Bingley would propose!"

Jane blushed, "Lizzy," she said sternly, but seemed pleased.

A DREAM OF THE SEA

*T*he moon shone over the dark and moving waters. Elizabeth slipped into the sea to hide her naked form, glistening in the moonlight. The water was warm and smooth, and she stretched out on her back to float with her arms spread wide, her hair floating about her head.

She exhaled, staring up at the moon and the stars. This was bliss. This was what she longed for: a quiet moment alone and away from everyone, in the natural world. The water cloaked her in darkness, and she felt herself slipping out farther and farther away from shore towards the moonlit horizon of unreachable possibility.

The splash startled her upright. She looked behind her and before her but could distinguish no-one in the dark waves. She shuddered as she felt a fish brush past her foot, then reached for the ground but felt only the watery depths.

She was farther out to sea than she had realised, and now she was not alone. A splash sounded to her right, and she spun around—but saw nothing. A splash to her left, and she spun again—and again, nothing but the waves.

The hair rose along her arms as she kicked away from the open sea and towards the shore. She heard another splash, and turned—for the last time, she told herself—to see the large tail of what looked like a picture she had once seen of a dolphin. The tail churned a swirling wave towards her as it swam out towards the horizon.

She paused, bobbing in the open water, kicking her feet slowly to stay afloat. Would she catch a glimpse of the creature again as it moved where her own heart desired to go?

The creature's tail splashed again, but this time it was closer to her. It turned towards the shore, and its tail propelled it towards her in the dark water. She gasped with wonder as she saw that it was not a fish, and it was not a man, but both— a merman of the sea, moving powerfully through the water, arms stretching for her. Her heart beat rapidly as she felt herself reaching out for him to take her, too, to carry her far out to sea.

His tail flicked again to propel him to her, and her body burst with energy. She thought she would move away, but instead she felt his arms encircle her as she reached for him eagerly, with familiarity. Now at this moment she did not know if she was herself or of the sea, a woman or a mermaid. A desire moved through her as their limbs entwined.

Time suspended, she reached up to put her hands into his hair, pushing aside dark wet locks. She knew this man, she thought as her eyes widened. But who could it be? Where had they met before? Was this a dream?

Her mind shifted groggily between the longing to continue dreaming and the bright flashes of the real. She looked at her companion's face, so familiar, hands encircling her waist, her fingers entwined in his hair, and she saw the face of the man she knew as Mr Darcy—Mr Darcy, holding her, caressing her, drinking in her eyes.

She thought she heard him say her name as their skin met

in the water, as she looked up into his eyes, dark and alive like the churning night sea, and found herself saying his name back.

Elizabeth woke with a start, gasping with shock and then relief.

It was a dream—it was only a dream. A thrill coursed through her, and she shuddered, closing her arms over her chest as she had in the water, though she felt inexplicably warm. She tossed and turned for some moments before deciding that it was hopeless to try to sleep again and managed to extricate herself from the bed without waking Jane.

She walked to the window, which opened with a slight squeak. A cool breeze blew onto her face, and she stood there for some minutes looking over the shoreline and the dark waves so much like the ones in her dream. She put her hands to her hot cheeks and nearly laughed. Him, a merman! Him— she could not even think his name—swimming with her in the open sea!

How could he have appeared so easily in her dreams? Her arms still closed about herself in an embrace, she tapped her fingers against her warm skin and thought for some moments. How could it have been his form, and not another, more pleasing one, who visited her in a dream? But was he so displeasing? In spite of all her justifications for disliking the man, he had done nothing of late but demonstrate an eagerness to please.

Why should he desire to please her? She did not encourage his continued regard. She breathed the crisp air, leaning her head against the window-pane. Everything between them seemed at an impasse. She had refused him, he had been angry, they had insulted each other. There was no reason to suppose that either expected or, indeed, desired a renewal of addresses. Now that she looked back on it, what she said during her refusal seemed very hard—too hard. Mr Darcy was not a man to take such effrontery lightly.

Was *she* the reason for his changed behaviour? She shivered in the breeze, although she still felt flushed. In her mind's eye flashed his unread letter, its three mysterious pages a weight on her heart. She could no longer deny that something of great import had been conveyed there, and he trusted she had read it. How she wished that in this instance she had let her curiosity guide her! For whatever had been revealed, she could then be content with her current situation and know what he was about. Then again, perhaps he did not know himself...?

Leaving the window open, she slipped back into the bed, turning this way and that as quietly as the sheets would allow. It was some hours of restless drifting before she fell asleep again; when she awoke, she told herself that she remembered a part of a dream that had been *something* to do with Mr Darcy. But she knew that it was nothing she *wanted* to remember— why would she?—or that she could convey to Jane or Mrs Gardiner, and so she willed the memory of it to fade away as the dark does at the coming dawn.

OVER THE NEXT TWO MORNINGS, IT BECAME APPARENT TO everyone in the house that something was the matter with Lydia. She was strangely subdued, sighing at breakfast and moping about until she was permitted to visit her friend Mrs Forster. Elizabeth and Jane were concerned over her frequent absences, but Mrs Bennet seemed to feel it to be in Lydia's best interest. Mr Bennet, for his part, did not mind being rid of her. Kitty was the only one who seemed able to account for her sister's behaviour and revealed to her aunt and sisters with enthusiasm that Lydia was in love.

Beyond this piece of information, they could unearth nothing. Kitty was very pleased with her secret and refused to disclose who was the object of their sister's affections. Mrs Gardiner, Jane, and Elizabeth discussed it amongst themselves with concern and made an attempt to corner Lydia so that they could understand her motives, but she laughed and said they were all a grand bore.

It was decided that it was only a passing fancy—and each was too busy with their own concerns to devote too much time to trying to understand the concerns of Lydia. Mrs Gardiner was consumed with her small children and their many excursions to the beach, Jane with Mr Bingley, and Elizabeth, as much as she loathed to admit it, with Mr Darcy.

There followed after this a period of several days during which Mr Bingley and his friend did not call at the house nor even meet them along the beach. Jane did not find this to be too distressing and bore her mother's flutterings with great forbearance.

"But we were all to go to the South Downs together for a picnic luncheon!" Mrs Bennet fretted to Jane. "How can we make plans if we do not know whether Mr Bingley is alive or dead?"

"Our plans are already fixed, as the carriage has been ordered," Mr Gardiner said. "We can go ourselves even if the gentlemen and their party are no longer attending. But why Mr Darcy would go to the expense of arranging a carriage—"

"Mr Darcy arranged a carriage?" Elizabeth gasped.

"You are always so shocked where that gentleman is concerned," Mrs Gardiner said with a smile, "when you know it can be nothing but a compliment to you."

Elizabeth could only shake her head when she realised that she shared the same worry over Mr Bingley as her *mother*. She feared that the time had come when Mr Darcy would guide his friend away from Jane. She feared that now there could be no hope for Jane and wondered that he had not put a stop to it before this. Not seeing him increased her anxiety at their meeting again—or rather, their never meeting again.

It was to her great surprise, then, when Mr Darcy arrived on the beach earlier than usual as she was walking somewhat removed from her father and uncle, who were playing another game of chess. She was reminded of the park at Rosings, and their frequent meetings there, and another moment involving the sea in her dream—but tried not to think too deeply upon it.

"Good morning, Mr Darcy, I was not expecting to see you," Elizabeth said as he offered his arm.

He exchanged the usual pleasantries, and continued thus, "You must have been wondering. He should have sent a card, but I am afraid he has been feeling too poorly to venture much."

"Mr Bingley?"

"He has come down with a dreadful cold."

"Oh, a cold!" Elizabeth felt a rush of relief. "What a pity that he should not have taken ill at Mrs Bartell's house. We could not have been happier to oblige him."

Mr Darcy began to laugh outright, and then quickly straightened himself taller, fixing a look of perfect respectability on his face.

Elizabeth blushed, realising what she implied, and attempted to recover, "I hope that all of your party have not taken ill?"

"All with the exception of myself. Georgiana only sneezes now and then, as she is of a good constitution, but I am afraid I must reorganise our plans for the South Downs until a different date—that is, if it is convenient for you and your family."

"I am sure my family will be most happy to oblige you. What a trial for my aunt if her children should come down with a cold. And no one would be able to hear me play over the sound of coughing, but that is of no import."

"It would be of great import to me," Mr Darcy protested, and Elizabeth declared him too gallant.

"You have never been given to flattery before this, Mr Darcy, I cannot account for it."

"Then your continued attempts to sketch my character have not been successful?"

"You change at every turn."

"Indeed," Mr Darcy seemed puzzled, but did not continue for some moments. "I should hope that in some respects I *have* changed."

Elizabeth looked up at him sharply and bit her lip before replying, "Yes, I believe you have." She looked away, not knowing how he would take this. But it was said kindly, and, she realised with surprise, it was meant kindly.

She glanced back to find him looking at her earnestly, an expression in his eyes that she did not care to interpret. A change of subject was in order, and she fumbled for her only ally: the weather.

"It is very fine out," she said.

"The clouds are gathering. I think it will rain soon."

"Oh, I had not noticed."

"Should you like to return to the house?"

"No, I like walking in the rain—" Here she stumbled, the image of his hair dripping with seawater flashing through her mind. "That is, yes, we should return."

Mr Darcy tried his best but could not help but laugh. "I see your father and uncle sitting over there," he gestured towards the rocks. "Should we join them first?"

"Yes," Elizabeth replied, breaking away from Mr Darcy and moving hastily towards the two. He was not far behind, his long legs exerting much less energy to cover the same distance.

"And so, Uncle, has he succumbed?" Elizabeth cried,

using the game as a way to distract herself from her embarrassment.

"Foppery!" declared her uncle in the most disagreeable voice he could manage, and Mr Bennet chuckled.

"Poor Edward. He does not know what he is about."

"We shall see who knows what." Mr Gardiner stared at the board.

"My father has had a run of good fortune these last three days, winning all their games. Uncle Gardiner is not pleased," Elizabeth said in a low voice to Mr Darcy, who took a stance looking over Mr Gardiner's shoulder.

"I once had the misfortune to lose every game for an entire year," Mr Darcy said solemnly, and the two older men groaned in sympathy.

"Bad luck, that," Mr Bennet murmured to Mr Darcy as his opponent made a move. "It must have cost a great deal of pride."

"Humility is not a lesson easily learned," came Mr Darcy's reply, and Mr Gardiner laughed with glee as Mr Bennet realised the brilliance of his move.

The players sat for several minutes in tense silence.

"No, no," Mr Darcy whispered to Mr Bennet, "not the bishop!"

Elizabeth disagreed with Mr Darcy. "Oh, come now! Would you have my father lose? The bishop is the best choice, Papa."

Mr Bennet looked from one face to the other and shrugged his shoulders a bit before moving the bishop. It was but moments before Mr Gardiner captured the piece and held the queen hostage.

"What are you about, Lizzy!" her father exclaimed, his brow creased. "I have never gotten a worse piece of advice from you."

She threw a challenging glance in Mr Darcy's direction. "You, sir, misled me!"

"I?" He feigned shock.

"Indeed. It was a suggestion laden with purpose; you knew I would disagree with you! You are hoping Mr Gardiner can break my father's winning habit."

"Why should you disagree with him for the mere pleasure of contradiction? I thought you above such behaviour," Mr Bennet huffed.

"You are vexed because now you are losing," Elizabeth retorted.

"No thanks to my daughter. Should you not be walking?"

"It is going to rain."

"The clouds seem to have cleared up a bit," Mr Darcy challenged.

"Then I will leave you gentlemen to your game." She walked off at a brisk pace towards the cliffs. After several moments, she turned with the expectation of seeing Mr Darcy follow, only to find that he remained with the other two gentleman, appearing to give advice on both sides.

She wondered whether perhaps he had only been waiting for an opportunity to be rid of her? But this would be a relief: it would not do to wish for his company. She did not desire it.

As she watched them, Mr Darcy turned and smiled at her, as if they were sharing a joke. She found herself smiling back, and with a shock realised that she did not hate him. She wondered whether she still even disliked him.

Though at first she admitted it unwillingly, his person had for some time ceased to be repugnant to her. Could it be that her feelings were now heightened into something of a friendlier nature? She shook her shoulders and gazed out over the sea, allowing her thoughts to be lost in the rhythm of its moving waters.

MRS BENNET WAS GREATLY DISTRESSED TO HEAR OF MR Bingley's cold. She resolved to send over a large package filled with her own remedies. Although Elizabeth found the idea absurd, Jane thought it pleasing and requested that their father send a note expressing the family's regret for the illness of their party. Lydia exerted herself so much as to suggest that a bottle of wine should be sent over as well, of which Kitty and Mrs Bartell both approved, though for very different reasons.

On the very day Mr Bingley and the entire party were declared recovered, Elizabeth herself succumbed to the cold. Although it was not much more than a sneeze and a cough, she was not permitted to stir out of doors for fully three days. When she looked in the mirror and saw the state of her swollen nose and eyes, she agreed that perhaps it would be best not to be seen in public, but that did nothing to soothe her agitated spirits. Elizabeth did not do well with staying indoors.

Jane was very kind and understanding, but their mother would not permit her to neglect Mr Bingley for long. Mrs Gardiner and the children often sat with her, read to her, and played games. But in the afternoon, they were always out at the beach, and Elizabeth was left alone with Mrs Bartell, who snored while she napped. It was in the small sitting room, with Mrs Bartell blissfully asleep, that Mr Darcy found her.

"I hope I am not disturbing you," he ventured, remaining near the open door.

"No, of course not," Elizabeth sniffed. "I would ask you to sit down, but I am afraid of your coming too near."

"I am of a strong constitution."

"I believe you, Mr Darcy, but, then, so am I!" She laughed, and he came forward to sit in spite of her protests.

"I hope you are not feeling too poorly?"

"I can withstand most things, but it is only with great diffi-culty that I can bear not being out of doors."

"I suspected as much," he said.

"You should probably not stay for long. Mrs Bartell is sleeping, and I am not meant to receive company."

"I see." Mr Darcy rose and looked disappointed.

Elizabeth felt sorry for his distress. "Thank you for coming." She watched with amazement as he withdrew from his pocket another shell, much like the first one she found.

"To match the other." Their fingers touched for a moment as he gave it to her, and then he was gone.

Mrs Bartell snorted and opened her eyes, "Was somebody just here?"

"It was Mr Darcy." Elizabeth gave her a reassuring smile. "He was here but a few minutes."

"Oh, I am sorry to have missed him. You were behaving with complete decorum, I expect?"

Elizabeth's eyes widened. "Mrs Bartell, if you are implying—"

"No, tsk," she waved her hands, "I did not think so, but one can always hope."

Elizabeth reached out and picked up the shell. "He brought me this."

"How very sensible of him. You needed another. I thought he would," Mrs Bartell nodded.

"You thought he would what?" Elizabeth pressed, hoping she would not drop off to sleep.

"Why," her head snapped up for a moment, "bring you another shell, of course. What else?"

"Oh, nothing," Elizabeth replied, but Mrs Bartell was already gently snoring.

IT WAS A HAPPY MORNING WHEN ELIZABETH AWOKE TO FIND her nose back to its usual shape, with only a trace of her sniffles remaining. Mrs Bennet was delighted. She had been considerate enough to wait for her second daughter to recover before arranging the date for the picnic on the Downs. It was difficult for her to be so thoughtful, but she felt that Elizabeth's presence was necessary to temper Mr Darcy's ill humour. She was delighted that she could now proceed with her matchmaking schemes without hindrance.

"I know how you detest the gentleman, Lizzy, dearest," she pronounced at breakfast, "but you seem to manage him well, he is in much better humour when you occupy him."

Elizabeth turned, and protested.

"Nonsense. I do not know why it is he bothers with *you*, but at least it keeps him away from Mr Bingley, leaving more time for Jane. You do your sister a great service."

Elizabeth covered her unladylike snort with a cough, and Mr Bennet nudged her foot under the table with a smirk. "He is a clever one, I think. We intend to add him to our small club of players, meagre as it is. His moves are not standard; bold, but effective. It pulls our unwilling minds into a forward way of thinking, eh, Gardiner?"

"Indeed, sir, but I will allow you the first game!"

"Elizabeth," Mrs Gardiner whispered to her after they finished breakfast and walked out into the gardens, "there can now be no doubt in my mind that Mr Darcy is a man of upstanding character. There must be something more to his dealings with Mr Wickham than meets the eye. Do you see it so?"

"My dislike for him, such as it…was," she replied slowly, "was not founded merely on the information of Mr Wickham."

"No? Then what, pray—"

"Aunt, please. My opinion of him has changed for the better, and in more ways than one. He is clever. But you should not suppose that our acquaintance is any more than it is."

"Lizzy—" Mrs Gardiner pursed her lips. "I think he is also

kind. While you were ill, he often met us outside on the beach. The children are so fond of him, and clamber at him on all sides."

"Aunt!" Elizabeth was mortified. "Surely he was offended by their exuberance."

"Do not distress yourself. He was surprised to be the object of such attention and does not seem to have much experience with children of such a young age. But he is very attentive to them. He went sea bathing with Mr Gardiner and the boys."

Elizabeth's cheeks flushed at this, pushing from her mind the hazy memory of a dream where she thought...no, she must return to the present. She had not thought of the real Mr Darcy condescending to sea bathe. But perhaps he found comfort in nature, as she did? Perhaps he was a good swimmer?

"Apparently he is an excellent swimmer. Your uncle said he swam out a full furlong. Lizzy? Are you attending?" Mrs Gardiner put a hand on her shoulder.

Elizabeth, who was still envisioning Mr Darcy moving through the water, shook herself back to the present. "Yes, Aunt. I have missed bathing in the sea."

"I am sorry that you should take so ill, and with only two weeks left in Brighton."

"I am sure it is Mr Darcy's fault," she said lightly. "For since he did not fall ill, he must have carried the disease about with him."

Mrs Gardiner laughed, "Is there nothing that is not Mr Darcy's fault? Was it not Mr Bingley who fell ill first?"

"Oh, no," Elizabeth joined in her laughter as Jane approached them, "Mr Bingley is all goodness!"

"What amuses you so?" Jane enquired.

"Lizzy blames Mr Darcy for her cold." Mrs Gardiner and Elizabeth burst into more giggles, but Jane seemed confused, and so the joke came to an end.

NEWTIMBER HILL

*T*he weather did not bode well for the day when they at last planned to set forth from Brighton to Newtimber Hill and picnic in the inland part of the South Downs. It rained steadily the morning before their departure and drizzled throughout the night. Elizabeth felt it reflected well her spirits, which seemed to be thrown into turmoil at any glimpse of Mr Darcy.

Mrs Bennet was not put off. Nothing could dampen what she felt was meant as a compliment to Jane, and she flattered herself by thinking that although it was Mr Darcy who extended the invitation, it had in actuality come from Mr Bingley.

On the morning of the excursion, the sun shone brilliantly. The large party included even the children and Mrs Bartell.

"Mr Darcy has hired a sedan chair—for me!" Mrs Bartell fanned herself. "I have not visited the Devil's Dyke since I was a young woman—about your age, Mrs Bennet—and I never thought that I should see it again before I died." Her eyes shone with anticipation.

As usual, packing for the excursion was an excruciating affair, with squabbles over the food and the bonnets to be worn. Elizabeth tapped her foot with impatience while she and most of the party waited for Mrs Bennet, Kitty, and Lydia. It was with pleasure that she was greeted by an unexpected visitor: Mr Walker, who had not been by as frequently of late as in the first weeks of their acquaintance.

"Why, Mr Walker! What a lovely surprise!" she said with a wide smile. "We are embarking on an adventure to see more of the South Downs today."

"I am a native of the area and must declare my heart's utmost devotion to the Weald," said Mr Walker, taking off his wide-brimmed hat. Elizabeth thought how prettily the sun caught golden glints in it.

"You must join us, Mr Walker," said Mrs Bartell, "for we have need of a guide, and there is no one as expert as you."

"I could not impose," he replied, and the conversation went back and forth thus until at last Mr Walker could no longer resist. Indeed, no one could refuse Mrs Bartell once she set her heart on something.

The journey to the South Downs took nearly an hour because of the poor quality of the roads, and, upon reaching Newtimber, everyone clambered out with anticipation. Everyone was hungry and declared themselves ready for a picnic. They arrived at a little hamlet called Saddlescombe, and there they met with the much grander carriage belonging to Mr Darcy and his much smaller and less cramped party.

Greetings were made all around, and Elizabeth marked the stiffness with which Mr Darcy and Mr Walker bowed to each other. She had not, as yet, navigated entertaining both gentlemen at once. She noted with some interest that Mr Darcy was much darker and a head taller than Mr Walker.

Mr Darcy had contrived to keep the details of the day's adventure a secret from everyone, and the youngest members of the party were somewhat dejected when it was announced that they must walk for another half hour to get to the top of Newtimber Hill, where they would picnic.

This provoked some rebellion from several quarters. Mr Bennet was fascinated by the many buildings in the hamlet but was satisfied when Mr Darcy said they might stop at Saddlescombe farm to see the donkey wheel on the way to the hill. Lydia complained of the heat and the lack of officers, but her older sisters sufficiently hushed her before she caused a scene. Mrs Bennet declared herself to be ready for anything as long as Mr Bingley was at her side and moved to take his arm. The other ladies fastened on their bonnets more securely and followed Mr Darcy as they walked with the promised reward of a picnic.

The party soon separated itself into several smaller groups. Mrs Bennet, unable to keep pace with Mr Bingley's lively step, soon found herself huffing along the road, leaning heavily on her brother's arm and complaining of the heat. Mrs Gardiner also hung back to help the nurse rein in the children, who were old enough to be exuberant but still too young to walk quickly. Mrs Bartell declared herself fit to be a queen in her litter, but the pace of her march was very slow.

The young people therefore found themselves at the front of the procession, with Mr Darcy and his sister out in front and Mr Bingley following close behind. At first, the older Miss Bennets and Mr Walker fell into step with Mr Bingley's two sisters, who tried to put on an air of civility.

"Dear Jane, Eliza! How wonderful to see you at long last," Caroline smiled through gritted teeth, and Mrs Hurst supported her sister's views profusely. "It is good to see your...*entire* family in such good health."

After a few short minutes of such tedious pleasantries, Louisa complained of the heat and slowed her pace, and Caroline stayed behind with her. Mr Bingley came by to offer Jane his arm and point out the wildflowers along the path. Elizabeth fell into step with Mr Walker, who began to discuss the history of Saddlescombe farm and its occupancy by the Knights Templar during the Middle Ages.

Soon enough, however, Miss Darcy hung back from her brother and walked over to join arms with Elizabeth. Miss Darcy seemed to be truly happy to see her.

"I am *so* glad you are come, Miss Elizabeth," she beamed, "for I always enjoy your company, and my brother has said that you are a great walker."

"Did he tell you, then, about the time I walked to Netherfield Park across the fields to tend to my sister Jane? I must have looked a sight with my petticoats six inches deep in mud. I am sure he would not want you to take *me* as an example."

"On the contrary! You are so kind, Miss Elizabeth, your affection for your sister is very evident. I should like to show such devotion to my brother."

"I am sure you already do!"

"My brother has also told me that you, too, play the pianoforte. I think that I love nothing more than playing the pianoforte—other than you, Fitzwilliam," she laughed. Mr Darcy was now close in front of them, looking back over his shoulder intently.

"Yes, my talents are many, but your brother and I may not agree upon what they are." Elizabeth saw that he was slowing to match his step with theirs.

"Oh, but I do! I have been looking forward to hearing you play for quite some time—Fitzwilliam spoke to me of your talents when he first came to visit after being in Hertfordshire. I have been instructed to extend an invitation to you and your family, most particularly, to dine with us. And then you will play for me?" Georgiana smiled.

"How can I refuse such a request?" Elizabeth observed that Mr Darcy was looking at her again, his brows drawn together. She realised that this was a scheme orchestrated between them.

Mr Walker cleared his throat and tapped Elizabeth's shoulder. "See over there, Miss Elizabeth, Miss Darcy." They first passed by a chalk quarry, and then stopped to gasp at the view of the large valley in the distance. "It is called the Devil's Dyke."

Georgiana shivered. "But why the word Devil?"

Mr Walker's eyes glinted in the way some people do when they have been asked a question they were longing to answer. "It is so called because the Devil himself was digging a deep ditch through the South Downs to use the sea to flood the Weald. But as he was digging, his shovel hit one of the rocks in the earth and it made a great noise. The clattering was so tremendous that it woke up all the people on the Weald and all the way to Brighton and they came and chased him away."

They waited some moments for other members of the party to catch up and then turned their backs to the quarry and walked uphill towards a large mount which Mr Walker referred to as the 'barrow'. At some point—Elizabeth was not sure how—Miss Darcy slipped away from her arm and attached herself, instead, to Mr Walker, who was pointing out the names of the flowers and the butterflies. This left Mr Darcy walking next to Elizabeth. He seemed, on this occasion, to prefer his usual silence, stealing glances when he thought she was not looking. What could he be about?

Along their route they saw more butterflies than Elizabeth had ever seen before. She stopped to admire a brilliant specimen on a flower.

"They look well together." Mr Darcy said in a low voice, causing Elizabeth to start.

Elizabeth followed his gaze towards Mr Bingley and Jane. She drew in a breath, and he smiled at her look of astonishment but said nothing further.

They walked farther up the hill, and she wondered what he meant. Could it be that his opinion of a union between Jane and Mr Bingley had changed? And in a moment she knew it to be true, for why else would they have stayed in company together for so long? Mr Darcy approved of the match! She knew it as if he had written it down in a letter. Suddenly her head was full of him, his eyes, his looks—the memory of his proposal rushing in as she thought of how he must have changed if he now approved of a match between Jane and his friend.

When they at last reached the summit, Mr Darcy declared that this was the place for the picnic. As the servants laid out the blankets and food, he offered his hand to help her down to the ground, her fingers shivering at his touch.

Elizabeth stopped to admire the rolling green hills. Far in the distance, because it had turned out to be a clear day, the hazy stretch of the blue sea was just visible. Her breath caught.

As the slow procession arrived at the picnic site, Elizabeth remained silent while people moved about her. Was he sorry for what he had done to separate Jane and Mr Bingley earlier? Was this his means of making amends? If he felt he was wrong in his estimation *there*, what of his other feelings? He could not approve of her connexions now—that could not have changed. Yet he seemed so fond of the Gardiners.

"Miss Elizabeth?" His voice broke her reverie. "What do you think?"

"I could not imagine a more beautiful balance of water and earth, Mr Darcy," she said, turning her face towards the sun and closing her eyes to drink in its warmth. She did not so much see his radiant smile as feel it.

The day was setting out to be a triumph. Mrs Bartell regaled the children with tales of the Devil's Dyke, though in her version it was an old woman with her candle who disrupted the Devil. Even Lydia, exhausted from the exertion, was sitting politely and talking with Mr Bingley about butter-flies. Elizabeth, worrying herself over dividing her attention between Mr Walker and Mr Darcy, now could not help but steal glances again and again with the latter, feeling her heart beat faster as she recalled the vision of him in her dream.

It was not until Miss Bingley spoke that the spell was broken.

"Pray, do tell me, Mrs Bennet, are the militia still quartered at Meryton?" she enquired.

"Oh, no, Miss Bingley." Mrs Bennet was only too happy to be addressed by the sister of the man she hoped soon to call her son and took it as a sign that things were tending in the right direction. "Surely you must know that they are here! In fact, my daughters, Lydia and Kitty—"

"Here, in Brighton! Good gracious," continued Miss Bingley, "what a comfort to most *everyone* here. What would you have done, Eliza, without the company of your favourite?" This was spoken in a manner that implied it was meant for the ladies' ears, but her piercing voice carried to such a degree that it was heard by all.

The group stilled. Elizabeth glanced at Mr Darcy. He did not look at her, but his head seemed to turn in their direction, his posture stiffening.

Mrs Bennet did not know better other than to reply, "Oh, you must mean Mr Wickham?"

Here Elizabeth rose in an attempt to prevent her mother, but it was too late. "Yes," Mrs Bennet said, "I am very vexed with him, for he left abruptly on business and has not returned. Elizabeth was disappointed, as were we all—but I never thought he was so attentive to *her* as to my Lydia. But you know now the Reverend—Mr Walker, just there—such a handsome countenance! He regularly calls, and I have great hopes of—well; one need not have only *one* favourite."

Elizabeth's mouth dropped open. She could not speak for

mortification. The silence was broken with a burst of coughing from Miss Darcy, who was turning red and had tears in her eyes.

"Miss Darcy, are you well? Georgiana!" Elizabeth saw her gasping for breath. She acted quickly, sharply hitting the girl square between the shoulder blades, and Miss Darcy coughed out the food that had been blocking her airway and fell into Elizabeth's arms.

"Can she breathe now?" Mr Darcy bent over them, his face white.

"Yes, she is breathing," Elizabeth reassured him, but Miss Darcy was still crying, the tears coming fast and hard.

"Oh no!" wailed Mrs Bennet, "Whatever has happened?"

Miss Bingley clutched at her throat. "Is she all right? What can we do? Louisa, Louisa—my smelling salts!"

Elizabeth wiped the tears from the girl's face. "There, there," she soothed, "You are well, you are well. Breathe now, breathe deeply."

"I want to go home," Miss Darcy cried, again and again. "Fitzwilliam, take me home. I want to go home. I cannot bear it!"

"It is all right, Georgiana." Elizabeth thought she must be embarrassed by the episode. "You are well."

But Darcy moved to sweep his sister into his arms and took her some distance from the group. They watched with worry, but soon Miss Darcy was set on her feet, leaning heavily against Mr Darcy, and they whispered to Mr Bingley. After some moments, the two Darcys started to inch back down the hill.

Mrs Gardiner rushed over to Elizabeth, taking her hand. "What has happened, dearest, is Miss Darcy very ill?"

"I do not know—at any rate she was most upset," Elizabeth replied.

Mr Bingley came forward. "It seems Miss Darcy remains

unwell, and Mr Darcy has determined to take her back to the inn and tend to her there. We can, of course, continue the picnic if we should so choose."

"Continue?" Miss Bingley gasped. "The very idea! We must return at once! We must catch up with them."

Mr Bingley stilled his sister from rushing back down the hill, but he could not prevent her from packing up. In fact, the entire party agreed that after such an event, to stay would be insupportable.

Elizabeth's own eyes blurred with tears as she stood up to make her way back to the hamlet. She told herself that—of course—she was worried for sweet Georgiana. She noticed, with great concern, that Mr Walker was speaking with some animation to Mr and Mrs Gardiner along with Mr Bennet, and she could not imagine what he thought to have his supposed intentions so blatantly and falsely proclaimed in front of strangers.

With some trepidation, she saw Mrs Gardiner approach her as they walked.

"Lizzy, do not distress yourself," she said as a tear slipped down her niece's cheek. "Your mother...I understand how you must feel, what it must seem."

Elizabeth could not trust herself to reply.

"Mr Walker is not angry with you, nor indeed anyone. Miss Darcy, I am sure will recover. But Lizzy, Mr Walker has taken this opportunity to—that is, he related to myself and your uncle and father details related to Mr Wickham that are shocking to say the least."

Elizabeth was not surprised. "What could it be?"

"That Mr Wickham,"—here Mrs Gardiner lowered her tone—"deceived those in his confidence and left Brighton in a great hurry because of his many debts. He had a reputation about the city of being a rake. I am afraid—I do believe that we have been spared much trouble by his leaving."

Elizabeth's head whirled, thinking back to his indecent proposal in the lane, and his hasty accusations against Mr Darcy. Mr Darcy! She had so misjudged him. What *were* the nature of their dealings, if Mr Darcy was not in the wrong?

It was at this moment of confusion that Elizabeth turned to see Mr Walker approaching and Mrs Gardiner smiling and moving away. Mr Walker offered her his arm, which she took with some mortification, having no notion of how she could manage to look him in the face.

"Let me reassure you, Miss Elizabeth, that I am in no way offended by you or your family this afternoon," he said gallantly, "I am sure all will be put to right. Indeed, I flatter myself to think that, perhaps, I *could* become a favourite…in time."

Elizabeth looked at him, his open and honest face so disarming, and took in a sharp breath. It was, perhaps, the kindest of all proposals (though it was yet not a true proposal) which she had received, and yet she could not see herself accepting it any more than the others. Another tear threatened to spill over her cheek, but she composed herself with another breath.

"I thank you for your compliment, Mr Walker, you are too kind. You are very good, but I cannot—"

"You need not answer me—indeed I have said nothing that requires an answer," the gentleman tripped over his words.

"Only I could give you no answer—not now, and not in the future. You must find another who could make you a favourite, for it cannot be me," Elizabeth said. "I am sorry for all the trouble we have caused you."

Mr Walker assured her that it had been no trouble, although his step was slowed, and they continued in silence for the remainder of the walk. What would her mother say now, when Mr Walker stopped calling? And what of Mr Bingley and Mr Darcy?

The entire party was in a state of depressed spirits until later in the evening when Mr Bingley himself came to tell the household that Miss Darcy was now in perfect health. His presence did much to alleviate Jane and Elizabeth's very real fear that their mother's speech might have broken something irrevocably with Mr Bingley.

So it was with some confusion that Elizabeth found the state of her own heart to be worse now it was not Georgiana over whom she was fretting. Elizabeth could not shake the feeling that she had lost something of Mr Darcy's good opinion of her—but why she should care for it, she could not yet let herself imagine.

IN VAIN DID ELIZABETH LOOK FOR MR DARCY THE NEXT morning. She waited first in the hall, then in the garden, and lastly on the shore. Mr Bingley came to call as usual, with all of his cheerful good humour, but said nothing of Mr Darcy.

"I know that he must loathe me now." Elizabeth paced along the length of the sitting room.

Jane was quick with her gentle reassurances. "Mr Bingley has not given me any indication that he—"

"Jane, how else could it be? That Mama should imply Mr Wickham was a favourite of mine!"

"Was he not?" Mrs Gardiner put in.

"I—no, well—that is of no consequence! Such a thing should never have been mentioned. And Miss Bingley! Such spite!" Elizabeth clenched her fist.

"You are angry, Lizzy. Perhaps you should take a walk," Mrs Gardiner suggested. "I am sure things are not so bad as you believe."

Elizabeth did not reply, though she recognised the wisdom in her aunt's suggestion. With a flourish she fastened her bonnet and stepped out the door, going towards the sea at a quick pace.

She knew now that there was something deep in the past between Mr Darcy and Mr Wickham. And she feared that she had been greatly deceived by the latter's tales of misfortune. How very improper of him to approach and ply her with stories of his woes!

"Miss Elizabeth?"

Elizabeth stopped dead in her tracks as she faced Mr Darcy, who sat on a rock overlooking the sea. She did not feel prepared to meet him.

"Mr Darcy," she said, her voice sounding curt in her ears. "I hope that your sister is feeling better."

His brows pulled together at this. "She is very well. I thank you for your concern."

Elizabeth opened her mouth to speak but did not know where to begin. Her first thought was to ask why he had not come to see her. But that would not do—indeed, what a ridiculous question. Her thoughts moved from there to everything, from asking him about Mr Wickham to a burning desire of knowing what he had written in his letter. Mr Darcy did not seem inclined to look at her, much less speak. Feeling tired, she chose to sit down next to him and then sneezed.

He offered her his handkerchief, "Are you well? Should you be out in this wind?"

"I am well, thank you," she replied, and the silence descended again until it became unbearable. She began again, "The wind is really not too strong, the weather has actually—"

"Forgive me." Mr Darcy rose. "I do not wish to speak of the weather."

Elizabeth could only blink in astonishment.

"Indeed, I cannot think why you should desire to remain here in my company at all, since it is, and has been since the day we met, so disgusting to you." He moved a step away from her. "I know not why you have allowed me to continue thus in my ignorance, but disguise is no longer necessary now that everything is out in the open."

"Mr Darcy, please—"

"No, there is no need to explain. Good day. I will leave you to your walk."

Elizabeth watched in silence as he went away.

THAT SAME AFTERNOON, IT WAS WITH SHOCK THAT A CALLER was announced to be none other than Miss Darcy, with her companion, Mrs Annesley. Some fuss was made over her appearance in the drawing room, with Mrs Bartell demanding her attention for a full twenty minutes before Miss Darcy managed to spill out her true intentions.

"You are all so very kind, but I came here with the express purpose of speaking with Miss Elizabeth," she said. "If I may…?"

Elizabeth, admiring her candour and curious about this revelation, led her out into the garden and away from the curious ears of her youngest sisters.

"It is a very pretty house here. The gardens are so lovely," Miss Darcy said as her fingers brushed against a delicate blue spray.

"Mrs Bartell enjoys the flowers. They keep her good company." Elizabeth attempted a smile, but it faltered.

Georgiana did not notice her discomfort and began abruptly, "You must have wondered at my illness the other day."

"Miss Darcy, do not—"

"You must call me Georgiana," she insisted.

"Georgiana, I have so many sisters and cousins, and all have choked at one point of another. I do know that my mother…well…" Elizabeth was not sure why what her mother said could have meant much to Georgiana.

"Miss Elizabeth, was Mr Wickham truly a—favourite? Of yours?"

Elizabeth sank onto a bench. "I cannot but answer you in truth. I thought him to be very agreeable."

"But you do not, now?"

"Since that time, I have become aware of his character—rather, his character has been called into question."

"Please, can you believe me when I say that he is not—he is not agreeable, Miss Elizabeth."

"My friends call me Lizzy. We are friends now, I think." Elizabeth motioned for the girl to join her on the bench, but Georgiana seemed too nervous.

"Fitzwilliam seems so troubled, I know it is because of—that is, I do not know what to do. He does not know that I am here. He would not approve."

Elizabeth put her head in her hands. "I am afraid I can offer you no good advice. I do not know what to do myself."

Georgiana hastened to take her hands. "Please, do not be so distressed, Lizzy!"

"I am sorry," she managed a smile.

"I am sure you could not have known that Mr Wickham was so—he is a villain. He cares for no one but himself. He is not concerned with love; he is concerned only with money. He deceived me, and deceived Fitzwilliam. He preyed upon my feelings and feigned an attachment, but with no intention…I am sure he must be spreading rumours about. I do not know what he told you, but—I was just fifteen—"

Elizabeth's eyes widened in understanding, the breadth of Mr Wickham's deception hitting her. "I believe I understand you."

Georgiana's wretched looks and inability to utter another syllable confirmed the dreadful truth.

"You need not say more, but you must be assured of my confidence. I think…I believe your brother tried to tell me but —" she paused, remembering his letter, "but I did not listen."

"I am sorry that yesterday, I—the comment caught me by surprise, that is all."

Elizabeth now understood. The shock of hearing Mr Wickham's name, not the embarrassment over her choking, was the cause of her distress. "My mother!" Elizabeth broke off, searching for words.

"No, no, your mother could not have known. And neither did Miss Bingley, although her attempt to wound you landed more forcefully on me."Georgiana sighed as she rose. "I did not want you to worry over me—I was startled, it is…it is painful to hear his name spoken. And then that you perhaps—I could not bear it! I had to speak with you to help you understand."

Elizabeth recovered herself and took Georgiana's hands. "You said you did not know what to do, but you have done everything right."

"You have been so kind to me, I could not help it."

"No, you have been kind to me, and I have done nothing to deserve it. Thank you for your confidence."

Georgiana did not reply but took her into an embrace.

IT WAS NOT UNTIL LATE THAT NIGHT, WHEN THE REST OF THE house was asleep, that Elizabeth sat up in her bed and began to cry. Despite her attempts to weep softly, Jane stirred at the sound of her sister's distress.

"Lizzy," she cried and pulled her close, "What is the matter?"

"Jane, I have been such a fool!"

"No, dearest, I do not understand."

"Neither do I, but I have been completely wrong! Oh,

Jane, I was deceived by Mr Wickham. I allowed myself to be! And now…now Mr Darcy thinks that Mr Wickham was my favourite, after everything he must have warned me about in his letter."

Jane stroked her sister's hair. "Lizzy, do not distress yourself. Could you not talk to Mr Darcy? Tell him that you made a mistake?"

Elizabeth quieted. "He does not wish to speak to me."

"I am sure he would listen," Jane spoke in low tones, stroking her hair. Elizabeth did not protest this and allowed herself to be stilled by Jane's soothing encouragement.

A MOST IMPROPER ELOPEMENT

*H*e rode out far away from the city to a beach not frequented by visitors or fashionable members of the *ton*. A wilder place—the exact sort that he knew Elizabeth would prefer above all others. Or had he imagined that, too? Her love of the uncultivated rolling hillsides, the rough-hewn rocks, the untamed Weald.

He would forget her, this time. Darcy tied his horse at a flat, grassy field before climbing down to the rocky beach, tugging at his cravat. If she did not love another, at least she did not love him. She had told him as much. He was a fool to think that he could win back her affection. Why should he break his heart open again and again in her presence, as if by standing there something would change?

He continued to strip, gazing out across the waters, the sun flashing as the waves broke. It was a good day for a swim. He waded until the water reached his waist and then with one motion dove under the water. Here, his battle was no longer with his heart or his mind but with the sea. He broke through the surface and stretched out, moving his arms in fast, even strokes. Cupping his hands, he felt the rush of the water as he pulled it past his body with every motion.

For a moment, he lost himself to that which he *could* conquer—the sea. He felt that he no longer swam but controlled the water as he moved through a current of his own making.

Then, he thought of her again—the hope of having her with him. He slowed his pace, treading water and breathing hard. She was, to him, unconquerable. She was one worthy of struggling for. To lose her was to lose a woman whose favour must be earned. For all that was his, she was not there for the taking. Giving in now would be giving in to what? A return to a life of pretension, to other women eager to please?

He surveyed his position, alone on the sea: the last man in the world, a floating speck against the great blue water that blurred into the sky. In the distance, he discerned a piece of driftwood some two furlongs away. It was far, but within his limits.

For a moment, the motion of swimming towards the driftwood was enough. It was his only goal. But soon, his desire to test his body blended with his thoughts of Elizabeth. For her favour, he tested himself and his resolve. If he could reach the driftwood, he could go back to her again. He could reach it. He threw himself against the waves and pulled, increasing force with every stroke.

THE NEXT MORNING ELIZABETH WOKE WITH NEW RESOLVE. She had greatly wronged Mr Darcy. All of her former dislike was turned topsy turvy. And now—she hated to think that he disapproved of her.

But more than this, her heart was flush with the strangest sensation—he who, she had been persuaded, was the worst sort of man in England, had been so eager to seek out her company, eager to solicit the good opinion of her friends, and was bent on making her known to his own sister. She felt... gratitude; gratitude, not merely for having once loved her, but for loving her still well enough to forgive all the petulance and acrimony in her manner of rejecting him, and all the unjust accusations accompanying her rejection.

Such a change she could only suppose must mean that he still loved her—ardently. This entire time, she had within her power the happiness of a man so changed and desiring to please, whose happiness might be changed by her. Did she want to be responsible for his happiness? Did she desire not just his approval, but his love?

No matter—she did not know if she still possessed any such power, or whether he might seek her out again.

"So, Elizabeth," Mrs Bartell said as they were sitting together on the beach, "You have finally come to appreciate Mr Darcy?"

Elizabeth threw her a faint smile. "Nothing escapes you, Mrs Bartell."

"When you are as old as I am," she croaked, "You will not allow things to slip past you, either!"

"Mr Darcy is—"

"He is very much in love with you."

"No, I do not think he could be anymore. I have been unkind to him."

"Perhaps in your thoughts, but not in your actions," Mrs Bartell chuckled. "You should see yourself when you look at him."

"I look at him as I would look at any other man!"

"Oh, no, not even from the beginning. You are drawn to him."

The memory of his eyes at her rejection, his face on Newtimber hill—the imagined sensation of his embrace in the waters of her dream—all burned through her mind. "He could not love me. I do not deserve it." Elizabeth rested her head on her knees.

"Do any of us?"

Elizabeth looked up and laughed ruefully. "No, I cannot say so."

"I am sure Mr Darcy has his moments of great stupidity. We all do, you know."

"I cannot say that he has always been half so agreeable as he has been here in Brighton!" Elizabeth smiled.

"But you know you must go to him if he will not come here."

"Mrs Bartell!"

"I am all seriousness," she nodded her head. "Time and love are delicate things to balance. Love does not like to be kept waiting."

"Love, Mrs Bartell," Elizabeth raised her eyebrows, "is something I am not entirely certain about."

"Are you not?" came her reply, and they returned to the house.

"LIZZY," MRS BENNET ADDRESSED HER SECOND DAUGHTER AS she chose a muffin, "you seem missish."

Elizabeth glanced from the tea things to the window, which displayed a fantastic downpour and scurrying passersby.

"Oh, I see, you want to imply that it is the weather?" Mrs Bennet scoffed and threw a knowing glance in Mrs Gardiner's direction. "But we know better, do we not, sister?"

Mrs Gardiner feigned to understand. "Come now, what is it you are about?"

"I cannot imagine what you mean," Elizabeth hoped to avoid a subject about which she did not want to speak.

"Lizzy is in love!" declared Lydia from the desk with a

giggle. There she sat, the picture of decorum, writing a letter. It was an unusual sight.

"Lydia!" Both Elizabeth and Jane spoke at once.

Mrs Bennet chuckled. "Which man is it then, Lizzy? Mr Walker? He is by far the better choice—with a living and..." Seeing Lizzy's face, she paused. "Oh, it cannot still be Mr Wickham? It is true that he was very charming—"

"—and handsome," added Kitty.

"—and *such* a fine horseman!" Lydia fanned herself to emphasise the point.

"—I am not surprised that you should miss him, but Lizzy, you should not expect—well, I am afraid the chances of your marrying are slim to say the least, my dear."

"Mama," Elizabeth's cheeks were flushed in anger. "I am not in love, nor have I ever been in love, with Mr Wickham!"

There was silence in the room for a moment until Lydia snorted.

"Mama, everyone knows that Lizzy is not in love with Mr Wickham—as if he could ever be interested in her!"

Jane and Mrs Gardiner threw her a quelling stare, but to no avail.

"Why, Mama, Lizzy is in love with someone completely different, and you will never guess who!"

"Lydia, there is no such person!" Elizabeth rose to face her sister.

"Indeed, there is!" Lydia laughed at her. "I shall write his name on this piece of paper!"

With a flourish of the pen, the deed was done, and Elizabeth lunged for the paper as Lydia brandished it aloft.

"Oh!" squealed Mrs Bennet. "Shall you not tell us, Lizzy?"

"Please, Mother," Elizabeth gasped as she leaped over Kitty to snatch the paper away from Lydia, who could barely breathe for laughing. She glanced down at the paper to see written plainly, *Mr Darcy*. "Lydia," she gasped. "How did you—"

"You are not very sly, Lizzy," Lydia said, and even Mrs Gardiner made a noise that sounded like something between a swallowed laugh and a gurgle.

Elizabeth threw the paper into the fire and sat down. Unfortunately, memories of throwing another paper into the fire came crowding in, leaving her flustered for a better part of the afternoon.

Only half an hour had passed since the thunderstorm when Mr Bingley arrived smiling upon their doorstep. He was received with as much graciousness as he was now accustomed to, and Elizabeth lingered for a moment to enquire after the rest of the party.

He turned and smiled at Jane before replying, "They are all very well, in excellent health. The ladies did not feel able to brave the streets after such a deluge. But Darcy," he added as Elizabeth sighed, "is in the gardens with your father and uncle. I believe a game of chess has been started."

"Oh—" Elizabeth jumped up. "Oh, yes, thank you, Mr Bingley," she replied as she left him to Jane.

Her coat, bonnet and gloves were all hastily assembled, and her slippers covered with suitable boots before she ventured out into the wet. A grey mist lay thin along the ground.

The gentlemen did not acknowledge her approach. Mr Bennet and Mr Gardiner focused on the board, Mr Darcy standing over them to observe the game. Elizabeth took her customary position behind her father. At last, in a reprieve, Mr Bennet looked up and smiled.

"There you are, Lizzy, we were wondering when you might join us," her father said.

Elizabeth glanced up at Mr Darcy. Had *he* asked after her?

"But it must be very tedious for you and Mr Darcy to stand

here while we play, for we have just begun. Sit over there and play a game yourself, sir. My daughter is a fine competitor."

Mr Darcy bowed solemnly. "If Miss Elizabeth does not object."

Elizabeth merely tilted her head and moved towards the other bench, taking the chess board from her uncle Gardiner's bag.

They spoke not a word to each other, Mr Darcy busying himself with setting up the pieces, and Elizabeth fiddling with her gloves in a moment of indecision. At last she pulled them off, for she did not want to play with them on. If Mr Darcy noticed, he pretended not to. As they both reached to straighten the last piece, their fingers touched. Elizabeth pulled her hand back, but not before catching his eye. A short disagreement occurred over who should play white, but Mr Darcy won without much struggle, and Elizabeth made the first move.

Her opponent sat for only a moment and then moved out his knight. Elizabeth moved pieces with rapid confidence, with Mr Darcy returning at a much more studied pace, until suddenly Elizabeth captured the queen. Mr Darcy sat up stiffly as if in protest but then relaxed.

"Well, it is of no consequence," he mumbled, "what use could a queen be to me?"

Elizabeth could not help but laugh. "Of what use could she not be? Indeed, she is the most versatile player, and can make the most moves."

"And therein lies her fault—for one can never know what she will do next."

"I do not know what you mean. I like her much better than the king. The king hardly moves at all, sitting there like a lump; and when he does move, it is in one step this way or one step that way. It is a wonder we guard him at all."

"A lump! Madam, have you never thought that the king

has much better things to do than fly across the board from here to there, never knowing where he is going. No, no, he is a thoughtful one, and does not make a move unless he must."

"What uselessness. To move only if one must."

"Perhaps it would be better to say he will move only if he is certain it will be to his advantage or to move away from attack. An active king is key to the endgame."

"And yet the queen is bold, sir. She is not afraid to do what she must."

"Not afraid?" His eyes met and held hers for the first time that afternoon, and suddenly her lungs felt constricted. "Checkmate, Miss Elizabeth."

Elizabeth looked down at the board and saw it was hopeless. "I am ruined forever, Mr Darcy. Papa will be displeased."

"Then I must beg your forgiveness."

"No." Elizabeth tried to laugh, but found she hadn't the voice for it. "I would not ask that of you. There is nothing to forgive."

She heard him catch his breath as he stood, and he looked at her with confusion. He seemed to struggle, and almost to speak, but then turned and walked over to the other men. Elizabeth, in her frustration, knocked over the chess set with her knee while standing, and, apologising to the gentlemen for the noise, gathered the pieces together and returned to the house.

THE NEXT MORNING BEGAN AS ANY OTHER. ELIZABETH ROSE early, walked, and returned just as the rest of the house was stirring out of their beds. It was not until five minutes through breakfast that anyone noticed something was amiss.

"Somebody is missing," announced Mrs Bartell, who had dined much earlier.

The sound of clattering silverware ceased. Mrs Gardiner

hastily counted her children and sighed with relief when they were all accounted for.

"No, no, Mrs Bartell, they are all here!" she called, but the lady shook her head.

"I did not mean your children, Mrs Gardiner, I meant Mrs Bennet's children!"

"Oh!" Kitty gasped, "Lydia is gone!"

Elizabeth turned to Kitty, "You must know where she is, for you two share a room."

"I...I do not remember her coming home last night," Kitty said in a small voice.

"What?" cried Mrs Bennet.

"I fell asleep!" Kitty began to wail as the chairs were pushed back, and everyone scattered to search the rooms in the house. Everyone that is, except for Mrs Bennet, who was waving her handkerchief about; Kitty, whose tears were dripping into the porridge; and Mrs Bartell, who was enjoying a piece of toast.

"She is not in her room!" said Jane, who had just come from upstairs.

"And not in the gardens," cried all of the Gardiners at once.

"Or in any of the downstairs rooms." Mary spoke as gloomily as possible.

"She is not on the beach." Elizabeth was the last to return to the room, and Mr Bennet moved to stand next to his wife.

"Where was Lydia last night?" he demanded.

"She was with Mrs Forster!" Mrs Bennet wrung her handkerchief and asked where her smelling salts were.

"Oh," Elizabeth said with a relieved smile. "She is with the Forsters, then. What is all this fuss about?"

"She was not meant to *stay* with the Forsters!" Kitty cried.

Mr Bennet and Mr Gardiner put on their coats and were just heading out when there was a knock at the door. It was opened to reveal a serious Colonel Forster and his distraught wife.

"Mr Bennet," Colonel Forster did not seem to know how to proceed.

Mr Bennet did not mince words. "Where is my daughter?" he demanded.

"I—is she not here?"

At this, the whole house erupted into chaos. The entire story came out, one word tumbling after the other. Lydia had been with them and was thought to have gone home. But that morning, when Mrs Forster had risen, she found a letter revealing that Lydia had run away. At this revelation, Mrs Bennet was escorted to her room, tended to by Mrs Gardiner and Jane. Mr Bennet's shock could not be contained. He paled and found himself led to a chair by Elizabeth.

"Why," she whispered, trying to hide the way her hands shook. "Why would she do such a thing?"

It was then that Colonel Forster found his voice. "It says in the letter that she has gone to elope—"

"—To meet with Mr Wickham!" Mrs Forster crumpled into sobs and threw herself onto the sofa, forcing Mary to bring her Mrs Bennet's smelling salts.

Elizabeth could not speak; she could only hold tightly onto her father's hand.

She heard her uncle Gardiner speaking sternly to Colonel Forster before saying a few words to Mr Bennet. Then, the Colonel and Mr Gardiner quit the room together in haste, leaving behind Mrs Forster and slamming the door.

"Lizzy," her father turned his eyes to hers at length, "What is to be done?"

"Oh, Papa," she cried and pulled him into an embrace, but she did not know what to do, either.

The next three hours were a blur of motion. Mr Bennet

removed to the library, refusing to admit anyone but Colonel Forster and Mr Gardiner. Elizabeth relieved Jane for some time of the care of their mother, and Mrs Gardiner questioned Kitty. It was quite certain that Lydia had left Brighton, but her destination was not clear. The letter, which she left behind for Mrs Forster, was read and reread several times. Her purpose was to meet with him, the man she loved, and they were to marry in the greatest secrecy.

Elizabeth almost tore the letter to pieces when she read Lydia's scribble announcing that it should all be a great joke. And then the house grew quiet. Mr Bennet and Mr Gardiner had left for London immediately, Colonel Forster's attempts from the morning to trace Lydia having pointed in that direction. After their mother was calmed, Mrs Gardiner, Jane, and Elizabeth sat for some minutes together in silence. Each felt the need for solitude, Elizabeth removing herself to the garden, and Jane to her room.

Elizabeth realised the true weight of her sister's actions. Lydia was ruined, and thereby her family. No one would connect themselves to a family in such disgrace. Mr Bingley might, but his friend would certainly not. Whatever his feelings for her had been, she knew that he could not abide joining himself to be brother-in-law to Mr Wickham!

And now, whatever chance there had been, if any, to renew his addresses, it was carried away by Lydia's foolishness. No, no, that would not do—by her *own* foolishness. The remorse which consumed Elizabeth was almost more than she could bear. She had known of Lydia's secret love and should have known it to be none other than her favourite. And Wickham had even proposed to her! Was this some revenge, had Lydia written to Wickham and told him of her sister's interest in Mr Darcy? Elizabeth sank onto the garden bench. She dissolved into tears, pulling her legs up against her chest and resting her head on her knees.

It was then that Mr Darcy happened upon her, and, seeing her swollen eyes, knelt at her side.

"Miss Elizabeth, are you well? You are ill, you should not be outside—"

"No, no, I—" She tried to move, but found she had no desire to. Mr Darcy's hands were on her arms, his face close in concern.

"I have been such a fool," she whispered, but Mr Darcy did not hear.

"You are not well, please, what is the matter? Is there nothing I can do?"

"No." The tears slipped down her cheeks, "There is nothing anyone can do! My father and Uncle Gardiner are traveling to London as we speak. Mama is—she is sleeping now."

Mr Darcy sat silently, waiting for her to continue. "Mr Darcy," she began, not able to look into his eyes, "it cannot be hidden from anyone. Lydia has—she has run away. She has gone to elope. And the man for whom she has given up everything is—" And here Elizabeth could not speak for some moments, until she voiced that it was Mr Wickham.

Mr Darcy turned away from her. "Is it certain that this was her intended purpose?"

"Yes, we have known she was in love for some weeks, but we did not know with whom. She left us a letter—she could not have left with such ease had she not been staying with her friend. I wish there had been some way to prevent it, some way we could have known—"

"There was nothing you could have done," Mr Darcy insisted, moving his hand to touch her shoulder, and stopped as Elizabeth burst into fresh tears.

"But you do not understand! If I had known sooner, we might not have come here—"

"I do not understand, you must have known, I—" and here he stopped.

"Mr Darcy, you will surely never forgive me. I am certain that you wrote something to me of him in your letter, but I—I did not—" she could not continue.

Mr Darcy rose to pace the walkway. "You never read it."

Elizabeth shook her head.

It was then that Jane came into the garden. "Oh, Lizzy!" Seeing her sister's face, she herself began to cry.

Mr Darcy stood in silence for some moments before saying, "I will take my leave of you, as I am sure you have been long desiring my absence."

"Goodbye, Mr Darcy." Elizabeth knew that he *should* leave, and that she was not likely to see him again.

Mr Darcy nodded and left the place quickly. The next news Elizabeth heard of him was that he and his sister departed Brighton the following morning.

A WILD GARDEN IN LONDON

his time, she knew it was a dream. She knew it like an ache in her chest, a knowing of the real world that was just beyond her grasp in the world of dreams. She knew it was a dream because she was in the sea in the dark, the sea that still called to her in waking and in sleeping.

This time, although she knew it was a dream, she could not mould it as she wished. She moved into the water again, swirling darkly about her—she was in her nightgown and she wrestled with it for some time to try to get herself free, the weight of it pulling on her body and robbing her of buoyancy.

Again and again, she kicked her feet to stay above the waves, which were increasing in their frequency. She struggled against her clothes and in spite of them swam out towards the horizon, where she believed that he would be waiting for her as he had been before. She called out his name in the darkness, not once, not twice, but three times. This time he did not appear, and she was alone in the sea.

MRS BENNET DID NOT EXERT HERSELF TO DRESS THE NEXT morning, nor the following. The Gardiner children were strangely subdued, though they knew not why. Kitty was a blubbering basket of nerves, feeling that the anger which should rightfully be directed towards Lydia had landed full on her. Jane and Elizabeth were both pale and drawn but collected enough not to cry. Mary bore it with philosophy, but her sensible admonishments were not received with as much relish as she would have hoped.

Mrs Gardiner was kindness itself and took care of everything. She soothed the depressed spirits of the two eldest, calmed the nerves of Mrs Bennet and Kitty, and listened to Mary with the greatest of patience. She urged her children to make themselves useful during this time of trial. The two older girls often brought Mrs Bennet's tea to her room and sat with her. The boys were too young to understand the gravity of the situation, but they took it upon themselves to amuse Elizabeth and Jane with somersaults and leaps off the divan. Their efforts were very much appreciated.

It was not long before Elizabeth noticed that they had neglected their hostess and hurried to Mrs Bartell's sitting room to discover what she was doing and apologise for their absence.

"Oh, pishposh, Elizabeth!" Mrs Bartell seemed affronted. "As if you should be looking after me at such a time. Despite what my granddaughter thinks, I am very capable of taking care of myself over the course of two days. I knew you would come around soon enough when things were more settled."

Elizabeth sat in a chair, looking dejected. "Of course I would come round, but nothing is yet settled. My father has written nothing. We have heard once from Mr Gardiner, and that only to inform us that they arrived safely. Mrs Bartell, I have not the smallest hope for her circumstances."

"It was foolish of her, that is certain. Not a good match, I should say. Mr Wickham is too flighty."

"Flighty is not exactly the word I would have thought to use."

"*You* were never observant of him, my dear. He was fidgety, something on his conscience. I daresay he is in a great deal of debt." Mrs Bartell nodded in her usual way.

"Nothing should surprise me at present. I no longer consider him a man of honour. Indeed, I dare say he has not the least notion of the idea."

Mrs Bartell merely turned her crinkled mouth into a half smile. "He may well have a notion of it and chooses to disregard it."

"He proposed an elopement—to *me*, Mrs Bartell—and just after he discovered that I met Mr Darcy. Even now I cannot understand his motives completely, only that he was hoping to revenge himself on Mr Darcy through me. But I did not even like him then!"

"I am sorry, who?" Mrs Bartell squinted in confusion.

"Mr Darcy!"

"Oh yes, before. No doubt you are quite right. Mr Wickham must have suspected that the mere proximity of Mr Darcy would help change your mind."

Elizabeth sighed. "One cannot think well of one without thinking ill of the other."

"But of course, Mr Darcy is so much finer to look at, it would not take long."

"Long to fall in love with him, you mean?"

Mrs Bartell began to chuckle. "Not long at all!"

"But Mr Wickham is considered by most to be the handsomer of the two."

"Perhaps if you prefer a boyish face. No doubt Lydia thinks him heaven and earth. Mr Darcy looks like a man."

Elizabeth blushed. "Yes," she replied, "He does."

Mrs Bartell's smile faded. "What a pity that he went away."

Elizabeth remembered their present circumstances. "Thoughtless girl! She could not think what it would do to her sisters, her family?"

"Your youngest sister is not one who likes to think—she likes to play. I never liked her at all."

Elizabeth tried to hide her smile at this and started when she heard the company bell. "Who could that be?" She moved to the window.

"Is it Mr Darcy?"

Elizabeth turned back forlornly. "No, Mr Darcy and his sister left town yesterday morning. I could not see who it was."

"Well, we shall have to go and look, then, shan't we?" Mrs Bartell began wheeling herself out of the room as Elizabeth hurried to her aid. They came into the hall just in time to see Mr Bingley enter. He did not notice their presence. He was staring at the figure of Jane, who stood motionless at the end of the hall.

"Mr Bingley," she whispered, "I thought you would not come."

"Jane—" Suddenly she was in his arms, "How could you think I could not return?" He stroked her hair and began to plant soft kisses on her head as she wept.

"Out, out," hissed Mrs Bartell, and with some trepidation Elizabeth wheeled them out of the room as discreetly as possible. Elizabeth's cheeks were flushed red, a thousand thoughts tumbling forth at once. Mr Bingley had returned to Jane! This was an unexpected turn.

"Well, how amusing!"

"Oh! He loves her, Mrs Bartell!" Elizabeth exclaimed, her eyes shining.

"Obviously."

"But my mother, I do not think she could bear so much at once. I should go to them."

"No, stay." Mrs Bartell placed a calming hand on her arm. "They will not do anything to further upset your mother, even with the happiest of news."

Relaxing, Elizabeth had just returned to her seat when she heard a pounding at the door. She flew up and, making a hasty apology to Mrs Bartell, rushed to the door. An express had come to them from their father.

Elizabeth called to her sister and broke the seal. Jane was immediately at her side.

"*My Dearest Jane and Elizabeth,*" Elizabeth read, her voice quavering with anticipation,

I write to inform you that we have located your unfortunate sister. She was, indeed, in London, and well concealed. They were found not to have any intentions to marry, but an arrangement has been made. They will wed before the week is out. Mrs Bennet will be displeased to know that they will marry from the Gardiners' house, but there is nothing else to be done. I would beg you to relate all of this to your mother, sisters, and Mrs Gardiner. She will shortly receive a letter of her own. I have not the heart to write more details, you will learn all soon enough.

Yours, & Etc.

Elizabeth sat down hard into a chair. "And they must marry, yet he is *such* a man!"

"Oh, but if they are to marry, they must truly love each other." Jane looked at Mr Bingley for reassurance.

"Jane, do not be blinded by your own happiness," Elizabeth said. "Why, it was only three weeks ago that he—" Here she paused, and Jane understood her meaning.

Mrs Gardiner's letter arrived later the very same day, and, though it was much longer, had no news of an extraordinary nature to relate. The time came to inform Mrs Bennet, who was still claiming grave illness, of this swift turn in her youngest daughter's fortunes. Whatever Elizabeth expected, their mother's raptures at the news of having her first child married could not be adequately described. Mrs Bennet went from distress of the acutest kind to absolute joy.

"A daughter married, and just sixteen!" She snapped at the maid to help her dress. "We must be away to London at once!"

"Mama, that is impossible—" Elizabeth said.

But her mother would brook no opposition, and, to Elizabeth's astonishment, Mrs Gardiner agreed with her.

"The burden on Mr Gardiner and your father at present is so heavy," she explained in a hushed tone to Jane and Elizabeth, "I cannot help but agree with you mother that we should return home today."

"But Mrs Bartell!" Elizabeth protested, "Her grand-daughter does not return for another week. We cannot leave her here alone."

"*You* must stay with Mrs Bartell, of course, Lizzy," called her mother, who had no time to listen for a response, for she was much too busy with other things.

"How shall you travel there safely?" Elizabeth was interrupted by Jane's returning to the room, pronouncing that Mr Bingley had offered his services to ensure their safe passage to London.

Elizabeth watched everyone scamper about for the next half an hour, until everything was packed and swept into the carriage. It was undoubtedly the hastiest preparation for a journey that Mrs Bennet had ever known, but she was determined.

"If we have forgotten anything, Lizzy, be so kind as to bring it with you when you return to Longbourn. That is, if we will be at Longbourn. We may stay in London, what a fine thing that would be! And of course I will tell Lydia of your heartfelt congratulations." Mrs Bennet managed as she pulled on gloves, cap and traveling cloak.

"Do not trouble yourself, Mama," Elizabeth replied, not unkindly, and gave her a swift kiss before she swept to the carriage, pulling along Kitty and Mary.

"Shall you be well, Lizzy?" Mrs Gardiner gripped her by the arms. "I will not go if you say you will not."

"Thank you, Aunt, I am quite happy to escape the confusion. But I shall miss you."

"And I you," her aunt smiled, and then allowed her children to clamour for their reassurances of affection before they all left to join the rest of the family in the carriage. Jane alone remained behind and held her sister in a tight embrace.

"Lizzy," she sniffed as a tear escaped her eye, "I am so sorry to leave you like this."

"Jane, do not worry over me. Please write, and tell Papa—"

"I will, dearest," she replied, and then was gone.

Elizabeth and Mrs Bartell looked across the hall at each other for some moments.

"Well." Mrs Bartell began.

"Well," said Elizabeth, and then began to cry.

My dearest Lizzy,
You may rest assured we are all well and safely arrived in London. Uncle Gardiner was happy to be reunited with our aunt, although I cannot say the same for Papa. He did not seem pleased at our arrival, having been prepared to leave the next day himself and carry us home.

attentive throughout the entire ordeal. I did not expect as much."

"*You* did not, but everyone else did. Why should you have doubted his constancy?"

"He demonstrated himself to be inconstant before, and too easily persuaded by—by his friend." Elizabeth looked down at her hands.

"Mr Darcy is protective of his friend? How charming."

"I did not think it charming, then," Elizabeth said with a half-smile.

"What have you heard of him?"

"Nothing—what does it matter? He is nothing to me now."

"Elizabeth, for shame!" Mrs Bartell pursed her lips. "You must always be honest, even to yourself. Of course, you *wish* he meant nothing to you!"

Elizabeth tried not to let her eyes fill up with tears. "I wish now—more than anything—that I had not told him of Lydia's elopement! He could have perhaps forgiven me anything but that."

"A connexion to the son of his father's steward?" Mrs Bartell coughed. "You, Elizabeth, have not thought this through. I cannot claim to know Mr Darcy so very well, but he does not seem the sort who abandons love for some such flippant excuse."

"I cannot be so optimistic as you are. It is also because—we quarrelled, before, and—the whole story is too long and ridiculous—he wrote me a letter, but I tore it up."

"Surely if you quarrelled it could not have been of great consequence. Probably one of those 'see what you have lost' sorts of arguments."

"I have no idea of his mode of expression—only that it contained important information."

"Have you apologised to him?"

"Not in so many words. And now I am sure I shall never see him again." Elizabeth returned her gaze to the downpour.

Mrs Bartell rapped her cane sharply. "Well! If he will not come here to see us anymore, then the only recourse is to *go to him*! Elizabeth, you must be off."

"Off?" She repeated, raising her eyebrows. "Mrs Bartell, if you are suggesting—"

She rose as the old woman nodded enthusiastically. "But suppose he is not there? What if he is at Pemberley?"

"Such details can be sorted out later, but now we must depart before my granddaughter arrives. She does not like for me to go to London."

"London!" Elizabeth exclaimed in wonder.

"London?" Came a voice from the doorway, and both ladies jumped.

"Amelia!" Mrs Bartell shifted in her seat. "Of all of the most inconvenient things!"

"Grandmama, are you feeling very well?"

"Oh, never better, darling," Mrs Bartell patted her cheek as Amelia bent down to kiss her before whispering to Elizabeth, "We will talk on it more tonight!"

Elizabeth did not know what to think but accepted Amelia's outstretched hands.

"So delighted," Amelia smiled. She was a pretty woman, not more than five and twenty and of a very small build.

"As am I," Elizabeth replied, "Your grandmother and I have kept good company for these two weeks. Although I dare say she will be glad to be rid of me."

"Nonsense," Amelia laughed, "she cannot stop talking of you in her letters! But what is it she is scheming about? Grandmama is always scheming something," she added in a whisper.

"Scheming," scoffed Mrs Bartell, "Don't you dare reveal our secret, Miss Bennet!"

"I would not dream of it," Elizabeth reassured her and, after a few moments of pleasant conversation, left for the solitude of her room.

Everything had been neatly stowed away that morning in preparation for her journey home the next day. The room was a picture of order and composure. But now, her heart would not stop beating fiercely at the thought of London and *him*. What did Mrs Bartell mean when she said to be honest with herself? And yet she had known, since the moment she heard of his departure, that she loved him. There could not be any other man so perfectly suited for her. The hopelessness of their situation had long been obvious to Elizabeth.

She had not doubted, until moments ago, that he could no longer love her—and there was no chance for forgiveness. London? It was a fantasy, untouchable, now placed within her grasp. She would go to London and somehow tell him that she loved him. He must at least know that.

Mrs Bartell wheeled into her room at eight o'clock that evening. "Amelia is in her bath. We leave tonight at midnight. It has been some time since I have done anything wild, much less running away, but I have not fallen so out of practice as one might think. Everything is arranged."

"Mrs Bartell, I do not see how—it is impossible for us to go to London after Mr Darcy. What if the journey is dangerous for you?"

Mrs Bartell snorted, "Gracious, child! Me in any danger! What is that to losing true love?"

"I do not think this will in any way help me find true love. It will only *reveal* my love."

Mrs Bartell seemed likely to say something, but then stopped for a moment. "I will not argue with you, there is no time. Be ready at twelve."

"I knew it!" Amelia's voice sounded behind them. "I knew that you were up to something—but Grandmama, you should not use me as an excuse to escape in the middle of the night. I am not the one who tells you where you can and cannot go."

Mrs Bartell protested for some minutes, and Elizabeth tried to reassure them both that she had no intention of putting Mrs Bartell in any danger.

Mrs Bartell took it upon herself to relate the whole of the tale, as she understood it, to Amelia, who listened with rapt gaze. "Of course you must go, but there is no reason to leave at twelve. You can go in the morning, like ordinary people, and spare yourself a great deal of expense."

It was in a sort of haze that Elizabeth found herself on the road to London the next morning, with Mrs Bartell snoring beside her. The coach rattled on, but Elizabeth could find no rest from the motion. Her trunks were all safely stowed, and she would be transported to Longbourn directly from town. In all truthfulness, she had no idea what she was doing or why she was doing it—except that she intended to see Mr Darcy and tell him the truth.

The distance was not very great, although with the dreadful condition of the roads, it took a few hours longer than usual to arrive at their destination. Mrs Bartell's carriage pulled up in front of a large house in a respectable area of town.

The housekeeper was shocked to see them. "Oh! Madam, I have not seen you for some years! What are you doing in town of all places?"

"Griselda, still as impertinent as ever." Mrs Bartell motioned to be moved into the house. "You are looking very old."

"Thank you, madam."

"Do not thank me, whatever you do!" Mrs Bartell laughed at her own joke. "Ah, Jonathan, here you are at last!"

A tall man with a long beard and spectacles came dashing

towards the women. "Mother! Have you run away from Amelia again?"

"Oh, Jonathan," she tried to be stern, but could not manage it. "It was a matter of utmost urgency. This young lady is my friend, and we are in dire need of sleep at the moment. We have an important call to make at the Darcys' tomorrow afternoon."

"The Darcys'? Mother, if you mean to—"

"Do not tell me what I mean or do not mean to do! Elizabeth, come this way," Mrs Bartell ordered, and Elizabeth, who was now more confused than at any other point in her life, allowed herself to be led to her room.

Elizabeth did not awaken until later in the morning, but she slept soundly and awoke refreshed. She ate breakfast along with Mrs Bartell just as her son's family was taking tea. There were many children, some grown, some young, scampering this way and that. She did not attempt to learn any names but surmised with amusement that Mrs Bartell seemed very fond of everyone though she couldn't seem to remember which name belonged to which child at all.

The moment came when it was time to return to the carriage and begin towards the Darcy home. It was then that Elizabeth's courage faltered, but with a deep breath and an encouraging pat on the hand from Mrs Bartell, she managed to climb into the carriage.

"Oh, it has been much too long since I came to this house," Mrs Bartell sighed as it came into view.

"You have been here before?"

"Yes, many times, but that was before Mr Darcy's father was born!"

"It has been some time, then!"

"If I remember correctly, there is a garden in the back of the house. Allowed to be almost wild."

"It could not be wild," Elizabeth protested, and then was silent as the carriage stopped.

They had just been handed onto the doorstep when another carriage, much grander than theirs, came round the bend and into view. Elizabeth almost turned round and hopped back into the carriage but was stopped by her amazement at seeing Lady Catherine descend.

"The lady herself! The very woman who caused my nephew to upend all of his plans for the summer! To stay in Brighton for weeks, when a party had been planned for Derbyshire." Lady Catherine approached regally. "Why are you here, Miss Bennet? And what do you presume—" Here, her eyes squinted as she gazed down at the form of Mrs Bartell.

"Is that you, Caite?" Mrs Bartell exclaimed.

"I—Guinevere! Is it really you?" Lady Catherine gaped.

"You are looking very old, my dear," clucked Mrs Bartell.

"And so are you!" came the quick reply. "What are you doing here?"

"I have brought Elizabeth. She needs to speak with Mr Darcy." Mrs Bartell peered up as Lady Catherine seemed to turn a shade of green.

"I cannot allow—I will not approve!"

"Of what?"

"Mr Darcy is not even here!"

"You cannot mean that—it is not becoming to lie. I put you in the corner for that once, if you remember. And look, here he is! The gentleman himself!" Mrs Bartell smiled, and Elizabeth whirled about to find herself face to face with Mr Darcy.

"How did you come to be here?" Without glancing at a beaming Mrs Bartell or a fuming Lady Catherine, his eyes locked with Elizabeth's.

"I-I came to see you!"

"But I have just been to Brighton and back to see you!" Mr Darcy looked down at his riding clothes as if to prove the point.

"Oh, why—" Elizabeth almost turned around as she felt her knees shake.

Mrs Bartell led Lady Catherine into the house.

"You know why. But why would you come to see me?"

Elizabeth's breath steadied as her fear melted away. She took his hands. "Because I love you."

In a moment, she found herself swept into the garden, which indeed seemed to have remained as wild as it had been some fifty years ago. Roses of white and pink tangled together on a stone wall, forming an arbor under which Mr Darcy drew her.

He put his arms around her. "You love me?" He leaned his head against hers. "Miss Bennet, I am afraid I require an explanation from you."

AN ENDLESS SEA

For a moment Elizabeth was lost to his eyes, his touch, holding onto his coat lapels and breathing to steady herself. "It is difficult to explain anything when you interrupt me so."

He tightened his embrace. "Do I interrupt you?"

"You certainly do," she replied with a smile, "but it does not follow that the interruption must be unwelcome." He let her go and stepped back a few paces. Elizabeth moved to a nearby bench under the roses. After a moment she looked down at her hands. "Can you forgive me for not reading your letter?"

"It is for the better. It was written in the most bitter of spirits."

"But I regret it. What trouble we might have been spared!"

"Do not blame yourself."

"It would be easier if you did not stand so far away." She reached out for his hand.

"I could not prevent myself from interrupting you if I stood any closer," came his reply.

"I wanted to thank you—" Elizabeth said, but stopped when Mr Darcy began to pace.

"No, no. No thanks. Who could have told you? I was sure your aunt was more trustworthy. Do not thank me, what I did was entirely—I thought only of you."

"I am flattered that you think only of me. But I was referring to your recent ride to Brighton in search of me. To what were *you* referring?"

Mr Darcy flushed. "Then you have not heard?"

"I am completely in the dark."

"Well, then, you may proceed with your explanation."

"Proceed?" Elizabeth exclaimed. "I cannot think now until I know all of the particulars! What could you have done to wish it kept a secret from me?"

"Please, Elizabeth, do not ask me, for I will not tell you."

She sat for some moments in contemplation, before gasping in realisation, "*You* brought about my sister's marriage! You have saved my family from certain ruin and ensured the happiness of more than one sister. How can I ever—"

Mr Darcy returned to the bench to sit beside her. "I attempted to dissuade Lydia from the marriage, as did your father, but it seemed to be the only recourse, for she would have him."

"I cannot believe it, that you would do this for me."

"I did not wish for you to know. I could not bear your gratitude."

"You have my gratitude"—she reached out for him again—"but you had my heart long before."

"And when, madam, was it first mine?

"I can hardly tell, it came so gradually. I do believe my heart was softened by your kindness to Mrs Bartell—but I did not realise how greatly I desired your good opinion until I believed I had lost it."

"I understand I am indebted to that lady?"

"Yes, I should not have had the courage to come on my own. But what sent you back to Brighton? I had no idea of your ever returning, even to Hertfordshire."

"The thought of your being there alone and unhappy."

"You knew of my unhappiness?"

"I have been to visit your aunt and uncle Gardiner yesterday evening."

"Oh!" Elizabeth laughed. "My aunt playing matchmaker! She was fond of you from the beginning. Is there any other detail which has not been explained adequately?"

"I am satisfied."

"Might I venture a question of my own?" He assented with a nod of his head, and she continued, "When were you first in love with me? How could you begin?"

"I cannot fix on the hour, or the spot, or the look, or the words which laid the foundation. It was too long ago. I was in the middle before I knew that I had begun."

Elizabeth lowered her eyes. "And was there a moment when you ceased to love me?"

"There were moments of anger and hurt. But I do not think it possible that I could stop loving you."

"Nor I you," she managed to say, before her lips were rendered entirely useless for talking.

"GUINEVERE, IT IS NOT POLITE TO SPY," LADY CATHERINE approached the window.

"I am not spying."

"You are spying, and you are entirely too meddlesome. I must protest."

Mrs Bartell snorted. "Must you always protest *everything*? Can you not see that they love each other?"

Lady Catherine gazed down into the garden for a moment, raising her eyebrows. "That is beside the point."

"Do not be so stupid, Caite. Things are different these days. These young people marry to suit themselves, as they should."

Lady Catherine moved from the window and settled on the divan. "I do not like her. She is impertinent," she sniffed.

"She is charming."

"She has no fortune."

"Mr Darcy will not be living with money, but with her."

"And what of Anne?"

"Oh, Anne!" Mrs Bartell exclaimed with a smile, coming away from the window, "I forgot about Anne!"

"Yes, well, now you understand."

"I am sure we shall not have any trouble finding a husband for her, Caite. Not if she is half so handsome as you were in your youth."

"Me?" Lady Catherine seemed almost to smile. "Yes, I was perhaps handsome, was I not? Everyone always used to say so. But Anne's constitution is so fragile, she has never been to Town."

"Catherine, did you not know? Sea bathing is *extremely* beneficial to one's health. You must send her to Brighton, and I will put her to rights."

"What are you two talking of?" came a voice from the door, and both women jumped in their seats.

"Nephew! When did you come in?" Lady Catherine exclaimed.

"I was describing the benefits of sea bathing for one's health," Mrs Bartell explained.

"Oh, very beneficial to be sure," he agreed, and the room fell into a sort of awkward silence as Elizabeth walked in.

"Well, Caite," Mrs Bartell said at last, "Do you not have something to say to Miss Bennet?"

Lady Catherine rose with the utmost of elegance. "Miss Bennet, being joined to our illustrious family is perhaps the greatest endeavour you will ever undertake. I do hope you understand the gravity of your position?"

"I will try my best to remember it, Lady Catherine."

"Yes, well, I suspect you will not. However," she continued after a poke in the ribs from Mrs Bartell, "I am very happy to welcome you into our family."

And here Lady Catherine condescended so much as to offer the lady her hand.

MR BENNET WAS NOT SURPRISED WHEN HE RECEIVED A VISIT from Mr Darcy to request Elizabeth's hand. Indeed, he wondered that Mr Darcy had not asked long before. The sheer happiness of Mrs Bennet upon learning that she was to marry not only one daughter to a man of good fortune, but two, cannot be adequately described.

Darcy and Elizabeth were married in the autumn, the very trees seeming to celebrate the union with their display of colour. Mrs Bartell felt it to be the very best time of year to marry, in spite of Lady Catherine's belief that no good could ever come of an autumn wedding. Both Mrs Bartell and Lady Catherine were happy to give advice often to the new Mrs Darcy, the new Mrs Bingley, and in truth, any person willing to sit and listen. Their thoughts on the subjects of marriage, love, childbearing, motherhood, the weather, and one's health, were, to say the least, extremely informative.

The reuniting of those two ladies brought about great amusement and new life to one, and to the other, an improvement of character. Lady Catherine and Anne became frequent visitors at the sea, and whether the latter's health improvement was the result of the sea bathing or of Mrs Bartell's insistence that she push her wheelchair, may be left for the reader to decide.

Elizabeth lay on the rocks, her eyes closed, the sun warming her face, when her peace was broken by a tug at her hand.

"Come, Mrs Darcy, the sea is calling." Darcy took her other hand and pulled her to him, her arms resting against his chest.

"Why Mr Darcy, how improper of you," the lady declared with a sly smile as she tipped her head back and kissed his chin.

He moved to take off her bonnet, and then let down her long hair. Reaching around to her back, he unbuttoned her dress with practiced precision. She rewarded his progress with kisses to help him on the way.

As soon as she was freed from her garments, she wriggled from his arms, running to the sea, laughing and turning to see him struggle to dispose of his own clothes.

She slipped into the water and swam quickly away, thrilled by her escape, looking to the horizon. The sun sparkled on the sea with a thousand glittering lights. She did not have to turn to know that he was behind her, reaching for her, and she turned to meet his embrace.

Their limbs intertwined in the water, and she liked to think how for a time they were one person there in an endless sea, their hearts open and freely giving of love.

She never could remember how many times they returned to the beach, for they visited almost as often in life as in her dreams. But even in her dreams, she never swam alone again, for he was always at her side.

Finis

The favor of your review would be greatly appreciated.

Subscribers to the Quills & Quartos mailing list receive advance notice of new releases and sales, and exclusive bonus content and short stories. To join, visit us at www.QuillsandQuartos.com

ACKNOWLEDGMENTS

First, an acknowledgement for the people in my life who keep me going. To Amy D'Orazio and Jan Ashton , who encouraged me to rework this novella. To my editor Justine Rivard, who helped me transform the material and embrace the sea. To Ellen, for a gorgeous cover. Thank you to my husband, David, who supports my endeavors and takes care of the kids when I run up against deadlines. Thank you, also, to my parents, brothers, and grandmothers, but especially Zach who pushes me to write.

Second, a special thank you my research sources. To my Uncle Bob, who grew up in Brighton and happily answered my 8 pm call to pepper him with questions about Sussex. I visited at 12, but details are fuzzy, and I could not possibly visit again at this stage of my life (not only am I tied up with family and work obligations, but there is a raging worldwide pandemic!). Thanks to my uncle, websites such as My Brighton and Hove (a people's history of the city: https://www.mybrightonandhove.org.uk/), the UK's National Trust (https://www.nationaltrust.org.uk/), as well as pictures and descriptions of hikers and travelers to this part of the world, I escaped the four walls of my Maryland home and journeyed to the seaside again—just the sort of wonderful thing for troubled times. Here, I hope that I have represented the spirit of Brighton authentically, even with some artistic license, and offer you (dear reader) a similar adventure.

Third, a heartfelt thank you to my friends, family, and new fans who brought and read my first novel, *Disenchanted*.

And lastly, a thank you to the teachers in my life. In particular, I want to mention my creative writing teacher, Ásta Bowen, who was the first non-family member who told me that I was a writer.

ABOUT THE AUTHOR

Kara Pleasants lives in a lovely hamlet called Darlington in Maryland, where she and her husband are restoring an 18th century farm in Susquehanna State Park. They have two beautiful and vivacious daughters, Nora and Lina. A Maryland native, Kara spent a great deal of her childhood traveling with her family, including six years living in Siberia, as well as five years in Montana, before finally making her way back home to attend the University of Maryland.

Kara is an English teacher and Department Chair at West Nottingham Academy. She has taught at the secondary and collegiate level at several different schools in Maryland. Her hobbies include: making scones for the farmer's market, writing poetry, watching fantasy shows, making quilts, directing choir, and dreaming about writing an epic three-party fantasy series for her daughters.

ALSO BY KARA PLEASANTS

Disenchanted

As a renowned wizard, Fitzwilliam Darcy thinks he is familiar with most of the spells, enchantments, and magic practised in the wizarding world. When he reluctantly joins his friend Bingley in Meryton, a small town not known for its magic, he is startled to stumble upon the rare gift possessed by Miss Elizabeth Bennet. The daughter of a poor country squire, she possesses a singular talent: she is not only immune to magic, but she can counter enchantments as well.

Despite their initial dislike of each other, the two draw closer as the threat from the Thieving Necromancer, a dark wizard stealing people's magic, grows more dangerous.

As Darcy battles nefarious wizards and Elizabeth unravels ever more difficult spells, they uncover dark secrets and break mysterious enchantments.

But love may prove the most important magic of all.

This Pride & Prejudice magical retelling contains the beloved characters of Jane Austen in situations and scenarios of the authors imagination.

www.ingramcontent.com/pod-product-compliance
Lightning Source LLC
Chambersburg PA
CBHW011442170626
46807CB00009B/3276

9 781951 033750